Amelia W. Truesdell

A California Pilgrimage

by one of the pilgrims

Amelia W. Truesdell

A California Pilgrimage
by one of the pilgrims

ISBN/EAN: 9783337286910

Printed in Europe, USA, Canada, Australia, Japan

Cover: Foto ©Andreas Hilbeck / pixelio.de

More available books at **www.hansebooks.com**

MISSION SAN CÁRLOS DEL CARMELO.

A CALIFORNIA PILGRIMAGE

BY

ONE OF THE PILGRIMS

AMELIA WOODWARD TRUESDELL

SECOND EDITION

SAN FRANCISCO
SAMUEL CARSON & CO., PUBLISHERS
1884

DEDICATION.

To the hallowed memory of one of the nation's grandest singers, whose words encouraged this labor of love, but whose own majestic numbers now know sublimer themes, this book is reverently dedicated.

INTRODUCTION.

The following pages do not purport to be a history of Missions, but only what the title implies—a visit to the old shrines. To local descriptions and legends are added such allusions to familiar events of Mission history as seemed desirable, with such fragmentary thoughts as would naturally be suggested to minds appreciative of the only bits of antiquity to be found in this new land.

The reader will remember that Junípero Serra was the first Franciscan missionary who came to Alta California. Having been appointed President of the future Missions, he arrived on the shore of San Diego Bay, with a few brother Franciscans and a small band of Spanish soldiers, in 1769. There he founded the first of those Missions, which, in turn, became the foundation of civilization on this coast. Soon after the arrival of the Spaniards in San Diego, Capt. Portolá, with a portion of the devoted band, started on an overland journey for Monterey. In their wanderings they came to San Francisco Bay, and claimed it for Spain and the saint whose name it bears. At various stations between the two bays, Missions were established, to which Father Serra devoted himself with unremitting fervor until his death in 1784. The work was then carried on by men inspired with the same zeal for God and the King of Spain, until a series of political changes, culminating about the year 1840, utterly destroyed the power of the Missions.

I questioned thus with the spirit:
  " O, how can I do this thing?
The pattern is long and hard," I said,
  "My thought but a slender string."

'O, faithless child," quoth the spirit,
  " Begin but to weave, nor doubt,
While the other end of the skein we hold,
  How can the thread give out?"

A CALIFORNIA PILGRIMAGE.

THE monarch of waters! the giant Pacific!
    How dwells he forever in kingly estate!
One mighty hand grasping the Orient hoary,
    The other wide-spanning the Golden Gate!
Rests his gaze amid scenes which are grand and eternal,
    The centuries' snows are a crown for his head;
Borealis, his torch-bearer, lights his state chambers,
    And the icebergs their flame-tinted canopies spread.

To his warm heart he presses his bride with her graces,
    Low responses she gives through her forests' deep chimes
To his wooing, in softest tide-cadences uttered,
    While their love-tale the minstrel winds bear to all climes.
High lifts she aloft the gigantic Sequoia,
    To catch on her brow the smile of his face;
And the moons that are whitest and suns that are clearest
    For ages have looked on their loving embrace.

California, bride of the princely Pacific!
    All humbly we gaze on the stores that are thine;
Not the gold that was torn from thy breast 'midst thy crying,
    But a greater boon ask from thy treasures' deep mine—
E'en a throb from thy life when thy soul was awaking,
    When the darkness was smitten ere dawned had the day;
When the light of the cross with the sabre's flash mingled,
    And the chaos of change in thy morn rolled away.

———

TELLS the cumbrous page historic how the Missions rose and fell,
    Founded by the Frays Franciscan—long their souls in heaven dwell!

California's Christian Missions, built upon an unknown shore,
Dark with tales of brutish native, bright with myths of golden store;

Tells how at the call of Spain, the Mother Church her paladins
Sent full-armed with holy weapons to the savage deep in sins,

The true faith to bear in haste as oil for wounds of holy steel—
Steel by Spain held pure when tempered in the fire of pious zeal.

How in wretched caravels the padres came from Mejico,
Churchly gifts and treasures bearing o'er the long waves dipping slow;

How when 'midst the dreary voyage storms hissed o'er the blackened sea,
Calm their *O Regina* mingled with that fearful minstrelsy.

How they came with toilsome journeys through the danger-crowded lands,
Where the cacti and the *mesas* kinder were than Indian bands.

Grieving not at isolation, save by it they lose the prized
Privilege of votive taper to some saint new-canonized;

How when, comrades close, among them death and hideous sickness were,
The *Viaticum*, though fainting, failed they not to minister.

FAIR as vale of Andalusia to their ocean-weary eyes,
    California spread her beauties 'neath a tent of cloudless skies.

Rich as Spain's oft-chanted *vegas* lay her valleys undefiled,
And recalled their own Nevadas, white Sierras far and wild.

To them seemed the mountain torrents, rushing down the cañons deep,
As loved Tagus or as Darro from Granada's rugged steep.

Spread the mother-land her banner, tarnished but still held with pride,
O'er the cross anear it planted by the mild Pacific tide.

Like the clutch of dying monarch was this final grasp of Spain;
Though with mortal home-wounds bleeding, reached she bold hand o'er the
    main,

Twisting in the young land's fair locks writhing fingers gaunt and old,
Hoping by th' electric current her fast-ebbing life to hold.

While upon Saint Isidore, the patron of the dear home-land,
Called the padres to extend to this shore his adopting hand.

And they christened the young giant in the true canonic way;
Saintly names their faith had given, children spell in school to-day.

Oft they met the cruel famine, and the hand of bloody deed,
Till the sprinkled blood of martyrs proved the Church's fertile seed.

But with miracles and wonders their discouragement was stayed,
When to turn them from their purpose Satan all his might essayed.

Soon their bells from tree tops swinging rung out *Glorias* to the hills,
And their chanted *Misereres* hushed the laughter of the rills.

And at length from cliff and cañon all the "little devils" fled,
Exorcised by Corpus Christi, forth in grand processions led.

All God's world rejoiced to help them; young trees lent lithe saplings strong,
Patient cattle died to give them supple skins for binding thong;

Mother Earth gave mud adóbe, and the sun his furnace heat;
Rolled the mountains their smooth bowlders; cold springs gushed for weary
       feet.

And they built aspiring turrets and arched corridors designed,
In a humble imitation of grand forms their mem'ries shrined.

Well their vines and olives flourished, and young herds flecked many hills,
Nature lavished on their efforts wealth from all her treasure-tills.

So the Missions strong and comely grew despite ungodly strife,
While the startled echoes wondered what should mean this unknown life;

And the valleys met each other with their leagues of harvest lands,
Till the broad and good dimensions linked the shore with priestly hands.

San Diego's level *mesas* on soft air the word sent out;
San Antonio, from the mountains, passed "Good cheer" with joyous shout;

Francis' Bay, on pulsing currents, told the tale from wave to wave;
Fair Sonoma's waiting hillsides backward cry of "Welcome" gave.

But the guile of their own sons and Mejico's bold hand of greed
Drove their flocks on devious hillsides; sold their lands for public need.

Poets sing and Christians sorrow o'er the wreck of good works done;
God looks on in awful silence, beams as bright His glorious sun.

———

TO the land of ruined churches fondly came a Pilgrim band,
    Grieving at the cruel blows by Time's iconoclastic hand;

Sorrowing for strifes of nations, and the feuds which end in guilt;
The insatiate lust for power that grasps what brother-hands have built;

Grieving for the sneer of scoffers, who pile scorn because appears,
Marred with trace of human frailty, toil of consecrated years;

Wond'ring at God's hidden purpose, at His patience suff'ring long—
That great patience which for ages views the strife 'twixt right and wrong.

Came the Pilgrims to the Missions, shod with zeal, faith's staff in hand,
Where they found them dead or dying, up and down the pleasant land;

Saw them bathed in morning sunlight—so false hope floods dying face—
And when noonday hazes round them burnt with a mirage-like grace;

On these ruins' haggard brows when twilight laid a pluméd crest,
Wooed they forth the Mission spirits with love's wand, aye heaven blessed;

For the souls of the departed seemed to haunt each hallowed shade,
As they were permitted guardians, at the shrines themselves had made.

As come hunted exiles shrinking, when the voice of Day is dumb,
From their haunts, where death-shades shudder, would the Mission-spirits come:

And they sat beside the Pilgrims, told their tale of joy and woe;
Of the Missions' cruel tortures, and their splendors long ago;

Of their swarthy children caught in grasp of a Briarian fate;
Of their final desolation and their present cruel state.

And the Pilgrims' hearts were smitten by such grief with pity sore,
Till they longed to tell the story to all people o'er and o'er.

On the mountain side south-sloping, and the *mesas'* lifted plains,
Thus they saw the pictured story, that which yet from death remains.

SAN DIEGO.

IN the College San Fernando, in the State of Mejico,
   Hangs a canvas dim with shadows thrown a century ago;

From it looks a monk Franciscan, in his order's robe complete,
Cowléd serge and hempen girdle falling to his sandaled feet;

With a rev'rent majesty he lifts on high the Crucifix,
Which tells Calvary's sad bequeathal to the chalice and the pyx;

On his face that confidence in holy work he had to do,
Born alone of such grand faith as *knows* its creed the "only true;"

Scintillant 'neath glowing faith, burns zeal as deathless and as bright
As the fire on Aztec temples through a fervid tropic night;

In his hand he holds a stone with which to beat his naked breast;
Near him lie a skull and scourge, and stands the chalice ever blessed;

Throngs his feet a motley crowd from many swarthy peoples led;
Tell their faces every terror; crouch they in all shapes of dread.

Such was Padre Serra preaching, as they say who knew him well,
Fray Junípero whose labors now but ruined altars tell;

He the man who consummation found unto his life's desire,
When in wilds of California, he might snatch poor souls from fire.

Whose rare ardor never failed, though tried by woes of land and sea;
To the glory of his purpose his great soul was ever free;

With his band he wandered long through Lower California's shore,
Where Tierra and confreres had planted good seed long before;

Where Ugarte, aye the bravest of a brotherhood most brave,
Built his "Triumph of the Cross," the first ship launched on western wave.

Serra, undismayed by mountains and the forest's unknown woe,
Onward went toward Colorado and the Gila's turgid flow;

Where De Vaca and Castillo, wand'ring to Pacific shore,
Healed the sick by sacred symbols full three hundred years before.

O'er the land where Coronado and De Niça sought in vain
For the seven-storied city—the Quivira of the plain—

Where two "Brothers of the Cross" had, near its fabled walls, laid down,
At the hand of trait'rous native, Calvary's sign for Zion's crown;

Places where the blood of martyrs should again bedew the land
By the blindness of the rulers and the Indian's red right hand;

Where the marigolds upspringing o'er the hasty graves should tell,
By a miracle of verdure, where the faithful friars fell;

Where procession of the murdered should pace o'er the blood-stained sand,
Each one bearing through night's darkness torch flamboyant in his hand,

While before them cross majestic, borne by unseen ones along,
Should cast such unearthly radiance on the chanting white-robed throng,

That they seem as flaming spirits, purging desecrated ground
With their versicles and incense, broken altars round and round;

Till these pagans, sorely frighted at the phantom night by night,
Should flee hasty leagues to southward from the weird avenging sight.

Serra thus all blindly wandered, dreaming not the stores of fate
O'er the place which should be later by his brothers consecrate.

Hence out-straying from his course to borders of the desert-land,
Where the cacti and mesquit yet mingle with the drifting sand;

Where shrink from the dry lakes sand-choked, e'en the bitter streams away,
And dead craters, with their burnt lips, lap the red sun's blasting ray;

Still they toiled the hot earth o'er, where sea-shells gleamed on waves of sand;
Swept o'er them the dread sirocco 'neath the fierce light of that land.

Lit the beautiful mirage strange mountains in their fevered sight;
Rose such walls as once on Patmos lay against supernal light;

Sprung tall minarets from temples tipped with balls of golden glow,
Casting spires of waving shadow on the bird-flecked lakes below.

"Feel we, sons, a woe to flee," quoth Serra, piously and well,
"Such the gleam of distant heaven to the souls shut up in hell."

Crossed themselves the soldiers dumbly, and though hearts were home-sick sore,
Pressed they on as sires and brothers had with vain hopes years before,

O'er the plains and rocky *mesas* where gray smoke-wreaths in the sky
Told of Indians stealthy lurking 'neath the cactus thickets high;

Up and down the land where Kino watched these lights with bated breath,
Land of silver, gold, and famine—land of mystery and death!

But the Blessed Mother watched and when closed deserts like a sea,
Rose 'midst sand and sage a portal graced by lovely family.

Matron fair as dream of morning, master grave but gracious still,
While a radiant boy to serve them hastened with a loving will.

There they supped, with loosened sandal, resting through the welcome night,
And thence passing, left a blessing fraught with peace as morn with light,

Beauteous boy, on them departing, looked with brow of splendor rare,
"Thus my father says the way lies"—pointing through the desert air.

When in pious speech they marveled how their hearts within them burned,
And constrained by love unresting, ling'ring glance they backward turned,

Lo! amaze! through sage unbroken, drifting sand-tides eddied slow;
Gone the friendly roof and portal with the morning's seething glow.

Knew they then that He had served them, who once washed His brethren's
feet;
Leaning on his staff then Serra worshiped in a rapture meet.

Toiled they on through Arizuma, land all wondrous winter fair;
But the spring-time's life had withered and the summer death was there.

E'en the hornéd toads had burrowed from the cruel sun away,
And th' alluring cliffs receded with their strip of shadow gray.

Onward, though the red simoon still sullen o'er the white dunes roll;
Spake the soldiers, "God in heaven! hath this hideous place a soul!"

Then quoth Serra, "Lo! the answer," pointing where their eager eyes,
Saw from whorl of spikéd cactus, tall white tree of blossoms rise.

Shaft, as marble of Carrara—graved as with a sculptor's care;
Carven tower of polished petals, graced with stamens waxen fair.

Spake he, "Children, let your lives be e'en thus rich in holy deeds,
Blooming in the fiery desert which would stifle common weeds.

"Aye! believe no heart so sin-burnt but Faith's seedlet planted there,
Shall bring forth in Love's warm sunshine, Hope's white blossoms late but rare."

Thus encouraged, toiled they onward, till from height of sea-girt shore,
Saw they tall masts upward pointing, telling their long journey o'er;

For the rude ships from La Paz, which sought Viscaino's Monterey,
Lay with sailors sick or dead in San Diego's close-locked bay.

Double-barréd gate as safe from pirate winds that roam too free,
As their stubborn faith from doubts which lawless rove o'er thought's high sea.

Placid bay! but bay resplendent when the broken shells of spray
Catch the morn and evening sun-pearls from the royal hand of Day.

Three moons Serra's friends had waited for his band they mourned as dead
Roaming o'er the coast and *mesa* where Spring's blazonry was spread—

Turquois stars and stars of sapphire laid she on her burnished green,
Fairy brooches fitly matching robes of every hue and sheen;

Champagne glass for elves' high feasting—white petunia's graceful cup,
Honeysuckle's conscious sweetness—maid too bashful to look up;

The ambitious pigmy thistles—tiny heads with plumèd hair;
And the oxalis white-petaled, with her nun-like grace was there;

Blue-eyed, meek forget-me-nots that never knew a lover's hand;
Wild sunflower—as queen barbaric that would wayside praise demand;

Censers all unblessed with incense—wild Eschscholtzias' golden bowls;
Rose they call Castile, from mem'ries planted deep in home-sick souls;

Thus in dainty heraldry, her legend in devices rare,
Bossed the *mesa*, Nature's 'scutcheon, crusting it with flow'r-gems fair.

Sick and dying, from their vessels came the Spaniards to such land,
But ere Serra saw it, ravished—shorn by Summer's scorching hand.

But naught quenched his deathless ardor, pealed his bells from scrubby tree,
Glad as if from storied turret, told they Christmas jubilee.

E'en when Famine stole among them, touching ev'ry haggard face,
And with Mutiny—the rebel—closed the hand in fierce embrace,

Never thought he of desertion, praying on with greater zeal,
Doubting not the end as certain—from God's word was no appeal.

When at length th' impatient soldiers, with their suff'rings reckless grown,
And despairing of th' "Antonio," storm-bound long in seas unknown,

Goaded fierce with cruel hunger, measure set for their delay,
Saying, "Leave we on Saint Joseph's, if she come not ere that day,"

All night at the altar lay he, till th' appointed dawn, when, lo!
Saw they by vouchsafèd vision in the clouds a good ship go.

Still prayed on th' undoubting Serra; when the fourth day nigh was done,
O'er the tide a ship bread-laden sailed athwart the setting sun.

All his life the grateful father, for deliv'rance of that day,
Celebrated mass memorial on the feast of San José.

And some tell that still is seen in San Diego's sunny sky,
On this day, through phantom clouds, a phantom ship go sailing by.

With that all-inspiring courage which urged laggards to their part,
Here began this man the labors so long cherished in his heart;

And they named the first young Mission for one humblest of the saints,
Eremite at tender age, when life her richest colors paints;

Didacus, the Andalusian, who came from his hermit cave
To serve Alcalá's sick beggars, eager life's worst ills to brave;

Who before the holy emblems fell in rapturous worship prone,
And whose form from earth uplift was borne by carriers unknown.

At the hour of his approach to hither-lying border land,
Roughest rope around his throat and holy cross within his hand,

And upon the crucifix his eyes that drooped 'neath gaze of Death,
"*Dulce lignum, dulces clavos,*" spake he with his latest breath.

Testified again the Spirit—e'en a dying prince was healed,
When within the royal chamber at his shrine the good priests kneeled.

But ere half-score years had passed e'en this saint's prayers had failed to stay
Satan's wrath and Indian hatred from a fierce and bloody fray;

For against the few thatched hovels came a thousand coward-bold,
Fought the Spaniards as their fathers in the holy wars of old;

And 'gainst torch, and spear, and arrow, consecrated carbine poured,
More inglorious than when flashed 'gainst scimiter the cross-hilt sword.

This the time when sat Vincente on the powder magazine,
Francis' robe the only shelter it and lighted torch between;

But that good saint ever watching, mindful of his order's fame,
Held from it the flames accurséd, that no spark anear it came.

Then rose Serra's master spirit, " 'Tis the Devil's final test;
Thank God, holy blood of martyrs proves the Missions heaven-blessed.

" By the soul of Brother Luis, sent hence without unction pure,
By his 'consecrated hands,' all that remained for sepulture,

" Build we more and build we higher, that the arch-fiend thus perceive,
Not his wrath can stay the blessings which the True Church shall receive."

Then was reared the once fair structure, which to-day a ruined pile,
Stolid sits upon the hillside, frowning at the valley's smile.

Frowning e'en upon the river, where the hill its current hems,
Shining thread of curling tinsel twisted round the olive stems;

Olives weird and ever moon-lit flecking all the plain with light,
Till the groining of their shadows mocks the artist's cunning rite.

Arméd cacti, as defending, by the garden wall now stand;
But the gentle palms, desponding, scarcely lift protesting hand.

Wide *potrero*, cattle-dotted, tells the Mission's ruined stage,
Where the padres strolled in converse through the *mesa's* fragrant sage;

Mesa fairest when spreads Twilight softest banners bright or gray—
Loitering mild-eyed *avant-courier* of the Night that spurns delay.

Gone all sign of churchly usage—gone the trace of padres' care;
Bells nor cross proclaim the story that His worship e'er was there.

Through the consecrated doorway, covered passes Vandal head;
In the vestibule adjoining, cattle make their nightly bed.

Not a saint nor altar standing; not a mural legend dear;
In the windows' deep embrasure dismal owls hold orgies drear.

Mass of sun-burnt bricks adóbe, half embanked in red decay;
Walls and roof proclaim the old curse—dust to dust and clay to clay.

Parent Mission, well belovéd! built in faith, baptised in tears!
Man sees only Time's fruition—God looks farther than the years!

L ONG the Pilgrims held sad converse, while night deepened round the shrine,
Till seemed lurking, guardian spirits in each dim and broken line.

Told they all the myths and legends each had heard from varied speech,
Twining old and new together that their truths the heart might reach.

What is this the rude foot presses! clinging leaf with vivid green;
Dew undrunk by thirsty sunlight flecks thy surface, sparkling sheen.

"Live-for-ever," children call thee! let the name for aye remain!
With the glinting dews upon thee, cover ev'ry blackened stain.

Grow ye lichens; grow ye mosses; cover marks of human strife;
Hope as dew on mould may glisten and from Death there cometh Life.

SAN LUIS REY DE FRANCÍA.

FAIR the "Santa Margarita" and "Las Flores" ranchos lie,
  Asking for their rival charms a smile from the admiring sky;

Bright their fields when with "The Flowers" spring-time dots their broad
    leagues o'er,
From the tip of rugged mountain to the edge of cliff-bound shore.

Here the grand old Don Juan Foster many years held princely sway;
Hence e'en to the Capistrano found his thousand herds their way.

Long dispensed he simple justice to a native peasantry,
Offering to friends and strangers patriarchal courtesy;

Oft the fierce *rodćo* saw he raise the dust-cloud on his plain;
Ne'er shall ring the mountains' echo with his bullocks' wrath again;

Flash no more the bright *seṛápes* of *vaqueros* on the hill,
And the wild bands' lessened numbers dumbly own the master will.

By the country folk belovéd, long revered will be his day;
For his soul still say they masses in the church San Luis Rey.

But before him, claimed the padres all the fair lands far and near;
Long their good herds fattened yearly on the sweet *alfileria.*

Wide these Margarita Mountains open cañons wild and deep,
Leading to San Luis Valley, then to eastward boldly sweep;

Low they crouch that o'er their shoulders Santa Rosa's head may rise,
Reaching for one dream-like vision of the sea-reflected skies;

Circling arms they interlace, till to San Luis' hills they reach;
These to westward, boldly stretching, hide the gleam of shell-bright beach.

Down the cañon runs the river—Luis called for kingly saint—
Winter current bold and rapid, summer stream with languor faint;

Ere its bent course meets the ocean, to a vale the hills expand—
Lonely mountain-circled valley, once the padres' pleasant land.

Here they built a stately structure on a southward sloping hill—
Castle with its guns commanding all the valley, wide and still;

Once "most splendid of the Missions," as the chronicle relates;
Now Destruction keeps each portal—Death e'en at the altar waits.

Here the noble Father Peyri, man of learning and of might,
Nearly two score years accomplished, loved by ev'ry neophyte;

Long swam converts by the ship which took from them his helping hand,
Pleading for his benediction and to go to his far land;

Man whose rare and varied powers Master's humblest service did;
But his heart with sorrow stricken, in his order's house he hid;

For his good work fell about him, by the hand of power smit;
But the angels keep the record where such labors all are writ.

Chose they for this Mission's patron, him of the benignant sway;
In the fair land which so loved him, "Good Saint Louis," still they say.

Once "most splendid of the Missions," and to-day its roods appear
In their utter desolation, than the Sodom plains more drear.

'Neath the roof of flaming frescoes to the wall a pulpit clings
And a canopy above it, like a bat with outspread wings.

In a chancel grandly lighted by a stately lifted dome,
Three great altars' tarnished splendor tells e'en yet the hand of Rome.

Here the soldiers made their barracks in the sanctuary's place;
Still the sacrilegious lines of target-marks the shrines deface.

When at games upon the altar, their audacious hands presumed,
Leapt forth holy flames indignant, and their gambling stakes consumed.

Battered saints, like wounded soldiers, watch the shrines they cannot shield;
Loving hands saved crownéd patron from this wreck, like battle-field;

Bore him to the friendly mountains, where a chapel owns his sway;
Where the neophytes' poor remnant still observes his festal day.

Not thus fled the King Crusader, when in Palestine arrayed,
Turbaned Turks before him trembled, by his banner's cross dismayed.

Now appears of former wealth but one old silver crucifix,
And at masses burn the tapers in quaint silver candlesticks.

Worship rarely wakes the echoes, burial service yet is said,
Marriage, baptism and the masses for the rest of faithful dead.

Then through high round arches springing from the frescoed columns nigh,
Weird old music throbs in anthems from the gall'ry old and high;

Indian voices and old viols—cadences which haunt the brain–
Drear as wail of ghosts returned, their own death-mass to chant again;

And the *Dominus Vobiscum* and responses dismal sung,
Meeting o'er the low-bent kneelers, hang like pall above them flung;

Till the prayer, the *Dies Iræ*, in the ferial monotone,
Sobs like backward drifting sigh of those who waited Christ's last moan.

But the curling incense rises with as subtle grace of line,
As e'er marked its spiral circles round La Sainte Chapelle's fair shrine.

Borne upon the chant's intoning, drifts it through the doorway wide,
Falling soft as benediction on the sleepers side by side.

L ONG ago man's greed for treasure undermined the sacristy;
Search as vain as hope of heaven, when to Mammon bows the knee.

Once most fair the dreary courtyard, where, above the fountain's play,
Shook its wilderness of shadow, *pimienta's* fern-like spray;

In the corridors adjoining, paced the priests at even tide,
Looking o'er the broken valley and their garden reaching wide;

Garden once of toilsome labors, miles of wall and arched gateway,
Tiled steps to a lake descending—lake deep-fringed with willow spray

Now a marsh where shrieking wild fowl come storm-driven from the sea;
Stalk the cranes 'mong cacti hedges—desolation's revelry.

One tall palm in tropic splendor—blessed where wrath on all is poured—
Lingers as last guest departing from a banquet's ravished board.

Unloved seems this lonely valley, wind-swept from the ocean near;
Rank weeds claim its sweeping acres; e'en its homes look dark and drear.

And the Pilgrims heard a legend which o'ercast the sacred place,
As might doubt of final mercy dim the light of saint-like face.

For 'tis said that godless aliens, on a midnight storm-hid quest,
Tore its paves for use unhallowed and its bricks for walls unblessed.

E'en from out the tabernacle, holy things in haste were borne;
Stood accursed the sacrilegious—scathed as trees by lightning torn.

And thereafter when black storm-clouds caught the stars from watching eyes,
O'er the garden's fringéd lakelet, noisome vapors would arise, .

Rise and shape to human figures, draped in penitential serge;
On their knees in dread procession, wrought they to the blast's wild dirge.

Semblance bright of silver vessels, some bore with atoning hand,
While weird light from cross and chalice lit the dark tile-laden band.

Up the garden's paved steps toiling—gate and walls no hindrance gave—
Resting not for rugged hill-side, till through desecrated nave

Passed they, laying on the altar what each thence had seized before,
While strove some, with bootless labors, walls and pavements to restore.

Rang their shrieks from castigations, self-imposed before the fane,
Through the dim church dome and arches, mingling with the wind's refrain.

And e'en yet the Indians whisper when lights gleam through blinding storms,
" 'Tis the spirits doomed to penance—look not on their curséd forms."

PALA.

CHAPEL OF SAN LUIS REY DE FRANCIA.

WHERE San Luis cañon reaches northward towards the river's home,
Six leagues from San Luis Mission still find Indians hills to roam.

High th' admiring mountains clamber each the other's shoulders o'er,
Gazing at the green sea valley from their cliffs of rocky shore.

Here is brooding silence broken by the ground quail's warning cry,
When he watches young flock feeding, breast white-ringed and proud crest high;

Plain-robed mother, through the sages, speeds her brood with cunning feet,
Then uplifts with whir pretentious far from safe leaf-hid retreat.

Here the flocks of black birds rising, whiz upon the morning air;
Far aloft the shy deer listens; to his covert bounds the hare;

Still dwell here the long-haired Indians in their smoky "'dobes" dark,
Squatting on the ground beneath their roofs of juatemóte bark;

Here the acorns and the pine-nuts, still they gather from the ground,
Pounding them in smooth stone mortars which in river beds are found;

Here they weave the graceful baskets strong with supple willow shreds;
And their granaries of young twigs, bind they with lithe *tule* threads;

On their heads the graceful *ollas*, poise they with a skillful sway;
Thin *tortillas* of the ground corn, bake they on hot stones to-day.

Here the Pala—Sparkling Water—springs forth with immortal birth,
Down the cañon greedy quicksands drink it from the thirsty earth;

And the natives fear to gather roots from near the living spring,
Lest from genii that dwell there curse of drought the act should bring.

Padres here built humble Mission, chapel of San Luis Rey;
Tropic plants and broken shadows, record of their work to-day.

Here the time-defying olive to the morn its slim leaves turns,
And in colors of the sunset, all its burnished silver burns.

Still pomegranates spread their blossoms, strangled by the tall weeds rank,
And the fruited Aztec cacti grow against th' adóbe bank;

Here the princely aloe raises penciled tree-top 'gainst the sky,
Rugged leaves, like faithful subjects, round their monarch abject lie;

Here was brought San Luis, patron, from his altar strife-defiled;
Hides he now his broken sceptre 'neath the mantle of his child.

One dark room of rough adóbe, roof where broken tiles gap wide,
Shelters statue of the monarch, once Francía's pious pride;

Crown as faded as his splendor presses curls beloved of France;
Royal robe about him gathered hides the warrior's broken lance.

He who built so fair a chapel, that the sun of France delays,
Its light arabesques to brighten, for the world's admiring gaze;

Chapel honored with the presence of the thorn-wreath *His* brow pressed,
And a "large piece of the true cross," with the healing virtue blessed;

He who came, a king uncovered, pressing earth with naked feet,
To receive the sacred relics and for them built altar meet,

Stands at shrine whose once blessed presence, bats' uncanny shapes defile,
'Neath a roof whose only frets are sapling boughs beneath the tile.

Loving Anthony stands by this altar of its treasures bare,
And fair Mary watches with them in a robe of silver rare;

And the rudest mural paintings decorate this dismal hall;
Wings of bats by cross and chalice; palms beside the arrows tall;

Consecrated walls defiled with pagan signs to Church unknown,
As o'er shrine some hand profane an unblessed altar-cloth had thrown.

One old tarnished copper censer lies upon the gaping floor,
And the few poor churchly treasures wait within yon creaking door;

Down this weird barbaric chamber flames the Virgin's silver dress,
As a ray of morn to wand'rers lost in some dim wilderness.

Sometimes now a godly father tells a mass in this rude hut;
Loose the rite on savage natures! dry husk on time-hardened nut!

Still their wizard incantations tell they at the mortal hour;
From the priest to wild magician, turn they for the healing power.

Here upon San Luis' feast there gather crowds from far and near,
'Neath *ramadas* of green willows, hold they wild and graceless cheer;

Indians and the Mejicanos try the games their fathers tried,
When the Spanish *caballeros* owned the land in ranchos wide;

In the ring the fleet *riata* brings the maddened bull to ground,
Cheers his mustang the vaquero—ring with shouts the mountains round;

From 'neath hoofs of flying ponies, buried chicken—hapless game!
Pluck they, leaning from their saddles; victor fairest maid may claim.

They, the pleasure-loving children, sons of idleness and songs!
From them slip their fathers' acres; unroused they by all their wrongs!

Comes each year a smaller number; as the tide from ebbing shore
Slip their lives into oblivion; soon the last shall come no more.

Undisturbed their sleeping brothers, though *fiestas* round them surge;
Though the rusty bells betoken marriage chime or fun'ral dirge.

O'er them stands a belfry tower, winter-stained and dark with moss;
On its crest one bird-brought cactus grows around the broken cross.

Lonely ruined tower of Pala! dark with shadows of the past!
Like Death's signet art thou set on shrines which must be his at last!

But from death comes resurrection; fertile fields wait willing toil;
Luscious fruits and grains life-giving hide within th' unnurtured soil.

Valley of the sparkling waters! soon thy hidden stores shall be
By the fair-haired Saxon stranger dedicate to industry.

SAN JUAN CAPISTRANO.

ONWARD from " Las Flores" rancho, following the shore-line steeps,
    Ten leagues distant from San Luis, 'midst the hills a fair vale sleeps;

Here the Coast Range, northward trending, opens in a tiny gate,
Where without, the chafing billows centuries for entrance wait;

And the Santa Ana Mountains, set in far transparent blue,
Gaze above the shrinking foot-hills on the sea the fair gate throug!

Here is hid a dainty valley, where two streamlets trickle down,
And the mountains warm encircle, bearing thorny cactus crown;

Where th' *arroyo*, called "Viejo," finds Trabuco's loit'ring stream,
And as young explorers seek they ocean-world's alluring gleam,

Stands the Mission Capistrano in a spot which well beguiles
From th' impassioned sun departing, all his hoarded farewell smiles;

Sun which flings each day new mantle, from his wardrobes in the west,
Mountain queen in splendor draping, patient feet and royal crest;

Spot which mildest moons illumine, where stars scintillating rise
With soft semi-tropic lustre—light unknown to colder skies.

In this calm and restful valley stands a shrine to one whose head
Knew no rest, when as Franciscan, poverty and war he wed;

He who from the Turks accurséd, strove to tear the shrines profaned
By the touch of infidels, and by the turbaned shadows stained;

Who before his crucifix, and all the faithful lances set,
Pushed the Ottoman's proud army and the star of Mahomet;

Who great riches, for the Master, with devoted life laid down,
Grieving he was "deemed unworthy" to receive a martyr's crown.

Blend the olive and the orange round his shrine their shaded green;
Tender bloom of gnarléd vines, tells boundless wealth that once was seen.

Dwells a padre grave and kindly—serves the people's humble needs,
Gathers in the oval olives, and the stores from fertile seeds.

Indians and the Mejicanos cluster round the brooding place,
Remnants left to tell the story of each dying, stricken race;

Tinkle the guitar and dice-box through the idle, dreamy days;
Castanets of the fandango tell the natives' careless ways.

Here long dwelt the same Don Juan who at San Luis Rey was chief;
Tell the Californians still his story with the words-of grief;

Of his free and wide donations—lands to strangers freely passed;
But 'twas naught to greedy Saxons; slipped his broad leagues sure and fast.

HARD fought Satan for this Mission; when foundation first was laid,
Told its buried bells and treasures long the Indians' threatened raid;

When at length returned the fathers, after many anxious days,
Gone the cross from place of burial; such Satanus' crafty ways!

Long they searched, till fell the darkness deep upon their hearts and brows;
Prayed they then and called the Mother, adding many fervent vows.

Soon before them in the midnight, with the grace of waving spires,
Burnt a lambent flame in beauty without touch of earthly fires;

Drew their steps its luring motion through the gloom by power unknown,
As a great love leads the soul in peace where darkest shades are thrown.

Dumb they followed where it skirted just above the honored ground,
Till beneath the spot which stayed it, eager hands rejoicing found

Altar marble and the paten gleaming in the darkness, bright;
Rang their chanted *"Deo Gratias"* through the arches of the night.

Sent the enemy thus baffled, emissaries of his own,
And the struggling young puéblo "robber-haunted" long was known.

Gliding to this dainty haven, pirates too held wassail nights,
Drunken from the Mission vintage; fled afar the neophytes.

Sought at length ambitious padres proud cathedral walls to raise,
That from dome of fitting grandeur might resound Jehovah's praise;

Years of Indians' doubting labor, by full faith their souls uncheered;
Stone on stone their fathers builded, stone on stone the children reared.

Cruciform the walls uplifted; massive arch and pillar said,
Vaunting, to the humble builders, "We shall stand when ye are dead."

Less than half-score years their boasting, when upon the Mother's feast—
"La Purísima Concepcion"—while the celebrating priest,

With the grace of broidered garments stood in ritual most grand,
And aloft the blessèd chalice held in his anointed hand;

And the low-browed converts kneeling, crowded all the tiléd floor—
Chants and incense circling round them, while their beads they fumbled o'er —

Heaved the earth like wrathful ocean; trembled ev'ry living thing;
Mutt'rings 'neath and crash above them, echoed back from wing to wing,

Down the heavy dome to pavement, downward bearing fearful death;
Passed the smitten ones to heaven, *Aves* on their dying breath;

For the Blessèd Mother, grieving at such fearful holocaust,
Freedom from the woes of Hades, gave as their poor souls out-crossed.

Smiled the sun upon the ruin; spread the sky as blue its span;
Who shall question God's eternal laws which know not works of man!

Cross themselves in pious horror, awe-struck Indians to this day,
Telling how their stricken fathers in the earthquake passed away.

Where the dread shock spared a chapel, priest infrequent mass now tells,
And the valley air still answers *Angelus* from sweet-toned bells.

Where the thousands lie forgotton, here and there a cross appears;
Say the unmarked graves to mortals, "Lo! the record of the years!"

Of those domes and boastful columns—of the roof and wall remains.
Pile of rocks and crushed adóbes, beaten by a thousand rains.

Sanctuary still is covered and the shadows tall and gaunt,
All its desolated niches like unrestful spirits haunt,

As if some from dust-hosts lying in yon ground, a penance held
For sins unconfessed or rash vows, as by spirit law impelled.

And they say that sometimes voices chant within this lonely shrine,
And at midnight spectral tapers round its burning crosses shine;

Melt such phantoms at the dawning with the shadows from its slope,
Gleams on it the morning sunlight, but for it no morning hope!

Soft 'gainst ocean's hoarse boom falls the hum of hours in idle flight,
As a picture's darker background brings the tender shades to light.

Mountain perfumes and sea-odors to a sweet narcotic blend,
And each day with languor ravished, slowly loiters to its end;

Till life seems an old man dreaming, and with evening's wond'rous glow
Flash the ruins as old faces gleam with thoughts of long ago.

SAN GABRIÉL ARCÁNGEL.

VEIL of the Sierra Madre! sheen of light to tell whose gleam,
    Earthly words opaque and dull-hued, as a child's clay image seem;

Sunbeams pale before the shimmer of the opalescent gauze,
Where the rainbow hue diffuséd, round Sierra Madre draws

Veil of glowing iridescence, woven from light's loosened rays
Smit by fine prisms atmospheric, in a thousand devious ways;

And methinks, when Spanish Fathers named the town Los Angeles,
That the grateful patron angels, loit'ring on the sunlit breeze,

Mantles dropped of heav'nly brightness, whose soft splendors never fail,
And they draped the Mother's mountain in their robes—this lustrous veil

Such the light through which Sierra looks towards plain of Gabriél;
Such the air which throbs responsive to its morn or evening bell.

All the subtle powers of nature, God's fine alchemists of old,
In this vale, as grand alembic, yield to man the purest gold;

Soft bloom, that seems air transmuted, flecks the clustered grapes with light,
Deepens on the downy umbels of the gardens, tropic bright.

Fair as Aztec princess wears the orange-tree her royal green,
Through lace mantle of white blossoms, golden jewels flash their sheen.

Haste the bees to sue her favors; for her breath the soft airs sigh;
Blushing bride and rampant childhood for her varied treasures vie.

Such the place by padres chosen for the patron angel's shrine,
Angel of th' Annunciation to the maid of David's line.

Farthest here once Mission farm lands spread o'er hills on every side;
Farthest roamed their good herds seeking food from mountain to the tide.

Most the Virgin loved this Mission, to her herald dedicate,
Near her vale as "Queen of Angels," where the "Mother's Mountains" wait;

Early she its cause espoused, when before her banner flung
Without hands upon the free winds—where a vision bright it hung—

Dusky warriors backward started, smit by grace of godlike mien,
As once Romans in a garden, back from face of Nazarene;

And the ones who came to slaughter, stayed strange worship to repeat,
Gifts from their poor riches leaving, with their weapons, at her feet.

Long the smile of peace thus given rested on the Mission young,
Till it grew to strength gigantic all its humble sons among.

"Once the richest of the Missions," now its desecrated feet
In *pueblo Mejicano* stand 'mid squalor of the street.

Here dwelt she whose oft-told story brings the tear of sympathy;
Who at six score years said sadly, "God must have forgotten me."

Kind to life, but no more loving; when the tardy messenger
Found her, eager to rejoin the swarthy tribes awaiting her.

Still a few old Indians linger squatting in the blazing sun,
Crooning of the Mission's splendors when *atóle* lacked for none;

And they tell of Padre Serra, crossing their brows at his name,
Tales of miracles their fathers told them of his holy fame;

How once lost upon the mountains came he to Mojave's plain,
Wand'ring with his people till the fever woke in blood and brain.

And through all the 'wildered journey told he ever wayside mass,
Though with thirst and famine fainting, ne'er without it day might pass;

That once from his trembling fingers, fell the cup of holy wine,
And with godless haste, the dry ground drank the crimson drops divine;

When lo! from the earth's parched lips, red with the stain of Precious Blood,
Sprang a fountain of pure waters, sweet as Horeb's smitten flood;

And when Serra with thanksgiving, would have done some penance still,
Spake an angel in a vision, "Nay it was the Master's will."

Crossed themselves again the speakers, lapsing to a broken dream;
Passed the Pilgrims wond'ring dumbly, what to them this life must seem.

ROUND this old church, dark and brooding, tropic hues their colors paint,
Bright as aureole around the pictured form of haggard saint.

But a tone discordant seems this shrine in symphony of light;
Have the Mother and the Angel from it turned their radiant sight?

Poverty and age are on it—for it can there aught remain
But to gather to its kindred—Gabriél on sunny plain?

In the graveyard all dismantled, honey bees find orange flowers,
Sweetness from the home of sorrow—thus brings time his kindest dowers.

Now appears but padres' dwelling and from church bell-tower shorn,
Broken chime still tells the story—"Christ in Bethlehem was born."

Still remain the riven walls with rough stone stairway standing nigh,
Roof restored spans lofty chamber, dim with light from windows high;

Cold stone floors reach musty chancel damp with air unsunned for years,
While the trace of many kneelers, in the worn square tiles appears.

From dark canvas look th' apostles, forms which knew a master's care,
Showman's rags draped round old kings, now their restoréd colors glare.

Stations of that way appear by which Jerusalem passed by—
From Sanhedrim to the rabble—mad to see the Christ-Man die.

Gone all trace of ancient altar, but stand new-made shrines for prayer,
And before the mystic symbols, pure light tells the Presence there;

But there lingers through this dark room echo none of sweet notes hymned;
Drear it seems as soul where doubts have faith and hope too early dimmed.

Slow upon the numbéd spirit creeps a horror in this gloom,
As if sigh from shrouded sleeper smote one wandering in a tomb;

And the shrieking engine startles all the gaunt shades with its breath,
As it were a fiend awaking those who lie unshrived in death.

'Midst this gray dusk watches still a group of saints on pillars old,
Faces dull and garments battered, names and sorrows long untold.

Stands San Gabriél, the patron, high above the other shrines,
E'en from face of faded statue, still some angel brightness shines;

He most honored messenger of all that stood before the throne,
When God would, unto His creatures, speak some purpose of His own.

He th' interpreter of visions to the captive prophet sent;
He who sat at Eden's portal, whence our "ling'ring parents" went;

Who came to the second Woman to announce the time as near,
When through her, th' Avenger promised to the first Eve should appear,

Whose high message, "Hail! thou blesséd in divine maternity,"
Lifted to the throne in heaven, pains accursed at Eden's tree,

Stands with ample gathered wings, as if he still were charged to greet,
With perpetual *Aves*, maid who stands enshrinéd at his feet.

Simple priestess-maid Judean! who should in thy humble place,
Deify to all the ages, mother love and mother grace;

Round this dreary shrine thy roses blossom in the month of May;
Light this gloom pale votive tapers, when is kept thy festal day;

Then the choir's soft *Incarnatus* trembles round thy vestal shrine,
As the new hope of the promise fluttered in thy soul divine;

And the eve's *Magnificat* breaks forth in glad triumphant tone,
As thy faith received the glory of the promise as thine own.

Maid "most pure!" maid "*gloriosa!*" woman with a loving heart!
Though thyself of mothers saddest, mothers' comforter thou art!

Patroness of every virtue! Almoner unto mankind!
"Queen of men and angels!" in thee, "Lady Merciful," we find!

Every grace, from royal sceptre to the shepherd's staff, wear'st thou
In the crown of many stars The Church has placed upon thy brow.

Pure impersonation of earth's sublimated joy and pain!
Of that love most 'kin to God's own, stand'st thou Mother of the Slain!

Motherhood beatified woke in thy canticle of praise;
Let the Æons antiphone it, till Time sees the end of days!

SAN BERNARDINO.

CHAPEL OF SAN GABRIÉL.

WRECK art thou beyond comparing, red clay pile of graceless shape,
E'en refuse the humble creepers nakedness like thine to drape.

Thou of Gabriél the chapel—brought by priests to goodly state,
By the same fond hands despoiléd—for rebellion devastate.

Long one strays with dreamful fancies that thy heart may whisper low,
Some strong thought for hopeful living from that life of long ago;

But such desolation palls one with a chill and nameless dread,
As if faith were shaken in the resurrection of the dead.

Sad we turn from longer musings, with thoughts like a heavy pall,
When anon a youthful Pilgrim climbs upon the broken wall;

Lithe of limb and supple sinewed, forth he stretches childish hands,
Where one spike of tender blossoms on th' adóbe ledge yet stands;

Gleeful shout and bound triumphant bid retreating footsteps heed;
Love and pride unite to bear this trophy of the daring deed;

As he lays the tender blossom on the waiting outstretched palm,
Its soft beauty, grown from ruin, breathes a peace like Gilead's balm;

Thus it murmurs—"Eyes of Mercy, than a child's more sure and kind,
In the worst wrecked life among us, may some trace of beauty find."

SAN FERNANDO REY DE ESPAÑA.

WOULD you breathe an air like nectar, fresh from heaven's vaults distilled,
    'Neath a dome of subtlest ether by electric currents thrilled,

Go to Valley of the Angels when the autumn morn is there,
While the sun's magnetic furnace seethes the aromatic air.

Here through noon's transparent azure, lights beyond it softly beam,
As a mantle's silver lining through its tissue web might gleam.

Where the mantle, earthward falling, wraps the mountain forms around,
At th' horizon's broken girdle, silver border trails the ground.

Here the mountains burn at sunset, with that light drawn from the skies—
Trail of glory drifting backward from the young world's sacrifice—

When the Bactrian high priest called to earth celestial splendors down,
And bade mortals worship fire as holy light from Mithra's crown.

In this valley host angelic floated 'thwart the ebbing day,
Sent to guide the fathers' search of shrine for San Fernando Rey.

Pointed they to distant mountain set in opalescent haze,
Where it looked adown the valley through the evening's crimson blaze;

Pointed they, then upward floated, and a cloud around them shone,
Soft as smoke of curling incense from the swinging censer thrown.

Burnt the moon as Real Presence o'er the shrine in heaven swung,
Lit the stars their altar tapers, fleece clouds as saints' banners hung;

Through earth's nave in grand procession—while God's glory round them
  burned—
Radiant host, for vesper rites, to heaven's lighted chancel turned;

The *Magnificat* exultant, whose high transport never dies,
Chanted to the Queen of Angels, floated downward from the skies.

When the Morn dismissed the night-guard from the border-land of day,
Smiled she to behold the fathers far upon their heaven-sent way.

Grieve all hearts that love pure labors, wrecking of their earnest toil;
Dumb the Pilgrims at the Fate which gives man's best to such despoil.

But the gardens which they planted, fairest here of all remain,
'Neath the mountain named for patron, Ferdinand, the Saint of Spain.

Olive trees still stand gigantic which a hundred years have crowned,
Triple avenues defining all the garden's widest bound.

To their peaceful arms presents its thorny breast the cactus tree,
And the noble aloes lift their coronets of filigree;

Closed within, a square protected shelter gives for clust'ring vines,
Rich in fruit the same gnarled trunks which gave the padres purple wines.

High among the storied olives, saintly palms their heads upraise,
And they mingle sighs together for the changed and loveless days;

Grieve they for the glebe unbroken, for the reservoirs long dry,
For the aqueducts where sere leaves in the tiny whirl-winds fly;

For the Christmas hollies redd'ning unplucked on th' *arroyo* bank,
Where, ensnarled with rugged willows, oily castor beans grow rank.

Grieve they for the life departed, for the ruined church hard by,
Where they see its cross no longer outlined 'gainst the cloudless sky.

Round the Pilgrims spicy incense through the yawning door-way came,
Burnt from cassia's yellow pastils by the sun's God-lighted flame;

But it fell upon no altar, for within is naught to say
What had been its hallowed usage, to the searcher of to-day,

Save the walls with broad marked columns, and the font's baptismal place,
Ornate with bold, gaudy pigments—efforts rude toward artist grace;

And the only chant that ever sounds within the dreary pale,
Is the fierce, hot wind of summer sweeping down this lonely vale.

Still without, the native houses cumber earth with hideous pile,
Wretched roof to bats and swallows give they yet a little while;

Stolid as despair an Indian dumbly crouched beneath a wall,
Genius of the past, awaiting freedom from the new life's thrall.

Words are not to tell the utter gracelessness of the combine,
Desolate as life despoiléd—drear as heart bereft, this shrine.

By the padres' house the peppers cast their quiv'ring shade to-day,
O'er the stony basins thirsting for the fountain's flashing spray

Loveless hands have desecrated with rough storage grown for years,
And with services of farm-life, till the tiled floor scarce appears,

All the corridor with arches where the padres loved to pace,
Looking down the tinted valley which their toils had crowned with grace.

Fair as Vega of Granada which her ballads love to tell,
Must have seemed to them this wide vale when their good fields prospered well.

Toiled they, emulating zeal of him whose royal life was spent
To redeem his land's perdition—Moorish "scourge for Spain's sins sent."

King loved e'en by foes who yearly came, a hundred Moors devout,
In procession bearing tapers, royal cenotaph about.

Spake the Pilgrims, " When this patron's armies scoured the Moro's plain,
Came no hope to his ambition, save the glory of old Spain?

"When he took Cordova's beauty and the gates of proud Seville,
With the pious sword and holy from the turbaned infidel,

"Came no dream, as angel blessing for such consecrated zeal,
Of new lands which yet should answer to the true faith's 'godly steel?'

"Land whose hills should lift from valleys where Spain's olives yet might grow,
Where pomegranates and lime hedges should in unknown sunset glow,

"Where the proverbs and the legends of the soft Castilian tongue
O'er the flocks and fresh-turned furrows should, 'neath other skies, be sung?

"Sought the land—achieved the conquest by that king's advent'rous race,
And the Moslem-reddened sabre found the earth's remotest place."

Spake one doubting, " Tell his story in the land he saw in dreams,
But old shrines and Spain's exotics o'er which th' unknown sunset gleams.

"Gone the Moors like comet stricken when the risen sun is nigh!
Gone the noon of Spanish splendor which eclipsed them in the sky!

"Gone the great and lesser glory, but both cross and crescent stay!
Who shall read aright God's lessons as He moulds the nations' clay!"

SAN BUENA VENTURA.

WHERE the ruins of Fernando's Mission far to eastward lie,
  And to west Saint Barbara still lifts the holy cross on high,

South-bent shore curves out a fair spot, sheltered by the coast-range near,
Looking towards the distant islands through the clear south atmosphere;

Air translucent, cheating distance of its boastful numbered miles,
Till spreads fairy land beneath us, cunning trick of nature's wiles!

Narrow valley here its wealth spreads e'en to ocean's fretting feet;
Yields this bit of earth to man, its lord acknowledged, tribute meet;

Sea-girt lies 'neath hills fantastic, bright with color but unclad
Save when winter—here a lover—spreads o'er them his shaded plaid;

And a stream from distant cañons, this vale with refreshment fills,
As a mountain scout that gathers good report from many hills.

Here was placed a Mission looking from the slope, a rugged guard,
Towards the sea which wakes the echoes with its deathless fusillade.

Heard the Frays, in lonely nocturns, billows break on silence grand,
Sound-waves 'gainst the mountains dashing, as the surf upon the strand.

Long this Mission for "Good Fortune" bore a name the whole land through;
As attested many guests, the patron to his name was true.

Planted fathers rarest fruits, with life of Spain's rich *vegas* fraught,
And on inward reaching *mesas* all their dusky toilers wrought;

Still on distant river banks, their pear trees tell the old, old tale,
And the fine roots of their walnuts find the springs that never fail.

Where the mountain valley, "Ojai," far below the sea-fog leaves,
Driest airs and rays sun-burnished gave them store of golden sheaves.

"Eagles' Nest"—this vale—an eyrie perched by Nature far aloft,
Trimmed with oaks and edged by mountains, lined with bloom and grasses soft.

Six leagues northward, in the narrow cañon of Matilija,
Where a winding passage opens towards Tulare plains afar,

On a little bluff projecting, one thick-walled *adóbe* stands;
Mimic castle of the mountains—it the narrow pass commands.

Here the idle Spanish soldiers, playing *monte* all the while,
Waited for the hostile Indians trailing down the steep defile;

And 'tis said that frightful goblins of the slaughtered savage foe,
Walk these ridges in the moonlight, when the burning north winds blow.

Where the children of the dark hordes claiming once these mountains high?
Scarce a score on distant rancho, toil they for a place to die.

Their good lands through Spain's hands passing, measureless from hills to shore,
Now from leagues to varas shrunken scarce protect the old church door;

And that structure, hoar with sorrows, sees its dearest mem'ries die,
Jostled by a thriving village where *rancheros* sell and buy.

Gone the padres' rambling houses with the picturesque façade;
Gone the weavers and the spinners from the square enclosed court-yard;

Unused lies the *Campos Santos;* lost is Mission garden ground;
Still a few old Mejicanos cluster the church steps around;

Now of olive orchards turning myriad gray leaves from the sea,
On the village streets ungathered, drops its fruit each straggling tree.

In a modern door-way two old palms historic bide their fate,
Calm and brave as princely captives chained within a hostile gate.

Thus remains of many labors but the church for use to-day,
Minding us of hands that reared it; dumbly asking, "Where are they?"

Vibrant throat of bells still calling, marks the *Ave's* hour for us,
From the turret named for saint who taught The Church the *Angelus.*

At this parish church a padre, with the stately mien of Spain,
Serves the altar and dispenses wisdom to his humble train.

Ne'er his closed eye nor his deaf ear turn to one of these distressed,
And his courtesy untiring, heeds the strangers' tedious quest;

Kindly shows he such church treasures as the Pilgrims' eyes may see,
And explains with zealous fervor his faith's questioned mystery.

Just within the wide church entrance from recess within the wall,
Copper font baptismal offers drops to cleanse from Eden's fall;

Mural frescoes in rude drawings, show the native artists' hands,
And a pulpit quaintly carven, pale in faded gilding stands;

Garish light from modern windows searches all the canvas old,
Where the story of the *Christus* 'neath the heavy cross is told;

Stands Ventura Buena, patron, priest and cardinal when young,
He the early-called by marvel, "miracles of grace" among.

Says the tale, "A saint from childhood," as was shown on dying bed,
When, by Francis' prayers above him, rose he as one from the dead;

When th' Assisan, spirit moved, of his great future prophesied,
Proudest mother of Italia, "*O Ventura Buona*" cried.

Words of omen well fulfilled, in wonder of his later years,
In which his humility e'en greater than his lore appears;

When he, kneeling at the altar, feared to take the Sacrament,
Lest his hand defile the chalice, till an angel, heaven-sent,

Held to him the Precious Blood—this bearer of the Holy Grail—
In the cup of song memorial—lost so long o'er hill and vale.

To the toiler of Assisi, friend-disciple, long he came,
Bringing store of learning's treasure to adorn his order's name.

Looks he from this old shrine, with a brave young face inviting strife;
Thus is Youth—it flings forever gauntlet in the face of Life.

From old pedestals lean saints whose names outlive neglectful years,
Toward the Virgin turning in mute testimony to her tears;

Stands an altar to Our Lady—she of Guadalúpe's fame;
Gracious hands she lifts unto us from an aureole of flame.

But the grandest decoration, 'mid designs of crudest art,
Is an altar of the Passion from the others set apart;

Ghastly Christ on rude cross lifted, while behind the clear-carved face,
All the symbols of His sorrow, on the wall your tears may trace—

Curséd rods and cruel nails that once were hid in holy flesh;
Crown of thorns and mocking palm-branch; spear that drew His life-blood
        fresh;

Sponge upheld in vile derision; robe of scorn they bade Him wear;
Chalice of the blesséd promise that His life, His own should share.

Mother stands and friend belovéd, 'neath the cross, with struggling tears,
Mourning in a long Good Friday, the fulfillment of their fears.

Meet the place for requiem masses which in holy week are said,
When the prostrate priest bewails the sorrows of the princely Dead;

When before th' uncovered cross he worships with the foot unshod,
And his chant's "Reproaches" rise as savory incense to his God;

Round this shrine the *Crucifixus* from the organ's dirge floats down,
Drear as once the noonday darkness fell on Calvary's three-crossed crown.

But at festivals returning, Christmas joy or Paschal glee,
Fresh young voices flood the dark nave with their tide of minstrelsy;

And the rippling sound waves sparkle 'gainst the Crucifix' dull gloom,
Bright as that first Easter sunlight flashed on Joseph's garden tomb.

What are names to hearts that love Him! one same hope is for us all!
Jesus lay within the dark tomb—grief for Him our common pall!

Why the strifes that vex the Master! the same themes our tongues employ;
Christ was raised from out the shadows—love for Him our common joy.

SANTA BARBARA.

SANTA Barbara stands fairest of the Mission shrines to-day,
  Looking from a rocky hillside where the mountain shadows play;

Here the proud peaks to the eastward call to those which guard the west,
"Ho! ye keepers of the sunset, make we here a place of rest."

And their brothers to the northward brace with sturdy rugged sides,
While the warm encircled foothills dip their feet in cooling tides;

And the dainty spot thus sheltered—jewel in a mountain ring—
Proudly as a fitting dowry, princess to her lord might bring;

Here the soft sweet airs distilling seem a necromancer's charm,
Wearied soul and body lull they till life seems a dreamful calm.

Looked the padres on the good land sloping towards the toiling sea,
Working waves of molten silver into fine drawn filigree;

Toward the isles—mirage-built castles—which light paints against the sky,
With a sunbeam for a stylus, dipped in more than orient dye.

Gazing from the Mission hillside, strangers pause to hear the tale
Of the ghosts that haunt these islands with their flambeaux far and pale;

For old sailors told the story, how at midnight they had seen,
When the blackened sky hung darkest and the sea took deepest green,

Phantom skiffs like *tule* shadows, and their rowers tall and stark,
Flit with torches 'cross the channel, through the hollow of the dark,

From the Ana Capa to the Santa Cruz' steep jagged shore,
And from Santa Rosa backward, through the still night o'er and o'er,

Back and forward to the mainland, to the Missions white and still,
Barbara's and far Ventura's faintly limned against the hills;

Long the rites upon the islands, as if there were celebrate
The returning day of burial of some savage potentate;

And the torchlights white and spectral swept the Indians' swart lines,
Till the shapes seemed ghouls of fable, feasting round some charnel shrines.

And the sailors held the omen to portend swift coming storms,
When the phantom flames thus flickered lambent round the goblin forms.

Where the list'ning Pilgrims paused to watch the distant billows roll,
Stood the padres, with their great zeal, grieving o'er each pagan's soul.

Looked they when the winter verdure draped with beauty outlines drear,
And the softened heart of Nature spake, "O toilers, rest ye here."

Built they when the spring-time brightened with star-flowers the rugged slopes;
Patron chose—a maid whose spring-time beamed with martyr's star-bright hopes;

And the Mission of their rearing lifts its comely head to-day,
Smiling down on resting valley, hills and town and sweeping bay.

Looked it once on countless Indians crowded in this pleasant place,
Now on blooming slopes and plain which Saxon thrift has crowned with grace.

See the fair and good proportions scarce defaced by Time's rough hand,
Corridors with Roman arches gracing cloisters where they stand.

Still within old aqueducts, the mountain's prisoned waters flash,
Reservoirs with goodly joinings hold e'en yet the fountain's plash;

Round it broken walls are crumbling, which but lend a rougher grace,
As a rustic frame which heightens beauty of a pictured face.

Walls of stone from pave to turret, strong as tower on arméd field,
Roof of tiles uplift to heaven—tiles the weight of warrior's shield.

Massive towers defend the portal, and the bells still tell their tale:
"God and truth go on forever, 'tis the faith of man doth fail."

Ent'ring through a great stone doorway, distant taper greets the sight,
Like a star of promise burning through life's sorrow-clouded night.

Here dwells half-score brothers serving—rise their prayers each hour of day;
One old priest untiring worships in true mediæval way.

Nigh a thousand score of masses he most piously has said;
True disciple of St. Francis—waits the crown his tonsured head.

Dim light from the small high windows, shrouds in gloom the outlines where
Slow appears a monk Franciscan, kneeling at a shrine of prayer;

Friar in a long gray garment, hooded folds of heavy serge,
At the waist with white cord girdled, heavy knotted as a scourge—

Five times knotted, to betoken honors first by heaven deigned
To the man whose tortured flesh was by revered *stigmata* stained.

Shadow-like he moves to greet us, and the rosary falls down
Where the naked foot in sandal shows beneath the heavy gown.

What is this revealed through gloaming! picture old a thousand years,
From Time's darkened canvas stepping, of the age when faith meant fears.

Spake he gracious words of welcome, and one started from the dream
Which the dim light threw around one, with its mediæval gleam.

With a graceful patience points he to what strangers come to see—
Arches, columns, and the walls marked with rude frescoes' tracery;

'Midst the pillars quaint old pictures, fearful scenes our terrors know;
Copies some, and some old masters, brought from Spain and Mejico;

Side altars to saints and martyrs where the faithful pause a space,
With an *Ave* breathed before the relic 'neath each sealéd place;

One is held in special rev'rence—here lie bones of little child,
Brought with signet of the "Papa" from the catacombs defiled.

Nero lies in earth unhonored, sceptre crumbled to the dust,
Maiden's mem'ry fondly cherished, write the Years their verdict, "Just."

'Neath this floor, stone-vaulted tombs hold old Castilian families;
Still the chancel paves are lifted when a Mission father dies;

With them lies the first appointed bishop of this western shore;
Hangs his sacred hat above him—mitre carved in panel o'er.

Unto Mary's shrine looks Joseph with his face of patience mild,
As of old in Egypt's refuge, watched he o'er the Maid and Child;

Round them, saints of many nations, bound in worship of one Lord;
Far above Saint Barbara, whose young heart knew the sweet accord;

She who from the great Origen heard the new faith's mystic lore;
She whose face graved on their shields, as charm 'gainst death, brave warriors
    bore;

Who from her three-windowed tower—where her father sought to hide
Intellect and rarest beauty he would place a throne beside—

Saw unmoved the flaming pageants of the princely cavaliers;
Wed her heart to heavenly bridegroom, to His sorrows and His tears.

When she smote, in godly wrath, fair idols from their pedestals,
And contemned their pagan beauty, which graced her ancestral halls,

To the judges this fair daughter, father gave with his own hand,
Asking he, of child ungrateful, executioner might stand;

When the glittering edge he impious, dared to lift o'er that brave head,
Outraged heaven spoke in horror, stood he in the act—stark dead.

As at this lone shrine Franciscan, her small relic rev'rence stirs,
So at grander altars stands she, "mentioned in four calendars."

Spreads within the sacristy young priest, with rev'rent pride, each fold
Of the vestments old and broidered, rich with symbols wrought in gold;

Shows he silver pyx and chalice; precious thuribles gold-lined;
Mite of True Cross fondly cherished, by Faith's eyes alone defined;

And old saints that stood dejected, as if from the altar cast,
Round a crucifix as saying, "True our love e'en to the last;"

Crucifix of cunning carving, where a matchless hand has shown
Tale of Olivet's grand passion, with a grace some master's own.

Such the vivid truth of line, the heart swells with a sudden throe;
Seems Gethsemane's low moan to throb once more through midnight woe;

Seems the cry of Calvary to ring through sounding years again—
Cry wrung from a soul's great anguish which surpassed all fleshly pain.

Mute with thought, through long dim cloisters, grope we to yon spot of day,
As our spirits blindly stumble through earth's doubts toward heavenly ray.

SANTA YNEZ.

ONCE Saint Barbara to northward reached afar her greeting hands,
O'er the mountains to a fair place in which sister altar stands;

Where the rugged steeps, San Márcos, look towards leagues of spreading green,
Held by rancho of San Cárlos, a *cañada* lies between;

"La Cañada de los Pinos"—wider cañon of the pines;
Place so named by poet-padres, "College Ranch" this age defines.

In a spot 'neath shading mountains where bright waters constant roam,
With her name for stream and hill-top, chose young Saint Ynéz her home;

E'en to-day her lands are comely—leagues to east and west they lie;
Rios and *arróyos* bring their life to plains from mountains high.

Still upon these cragged slopes the deer feed in the twilight glow,
While the bear and pigmy lion keep at bay the common foe.

Here Madroño, masquerader, makes the shrubby forest gay;
Hangs the Manzanita shyly, berries bright by mountain way.

On the creeks the plant of Gilead finds the bay's funereal tree;
Heaven's healing on Death's footstep follows, if we will but see.

Of these hills the herds unconquered, ownership with grizzlies claimed,
Ruled the bullock o'er the mountain, as some savage prince untamed.

Often here the wild *rodéo* tore the dust from ev'ry hill,
And the bellowing of cattle made the very tree-tops thrill.

Proud rode forth the brave *vaquero*, horse and rider moved as one,
Pawed the ground th' impatient mustang, eager for the fray begun.

Dashed they in 'mong fierce bands surging, wild as billows winter-lashed;
Like white boats o'er waves wind-driven, their sun-bright *sombreros* flashed;

Parting rightward, parting leftward, that each ranch its own might gain;
Savage bullocks with their wide horns, plowed the trembling earth in vain;

For the hissing keen *riatas'* level circles small or great,
Seized upon the maddened captives, like a fierce pursuing fate;

Supple dropped on horns defiant, sinuous caught the flying feet;
Swayed each rider in his saddle, with a movement bold and fleet;

Backward braced the foaming mustang, rolled the conquered to the ground,
Helpless 'neath the branding iron, firmly by the skilled noose bound.

Gone the wild herds from the mountains; ride forth few *vaqueros* now;
Hang the braided lithe *riatas* useless on the saddle-bow;

For the droves in paltry numbers, tame as barn-yard bovines stand,
In their bondage scarce rebelling at the hot iron's servile brand.

———

WHERE the mountain's veil is bluest, like bones bleaching in the sun,
    Lie stark ruins of the work built late ere padres' time was done;

Mission young when Anarchy its night spread o'er the fair south land;
'Midst the gloom its tender life was strangled by Might's ruthless hand.

Guards this shrine one aged Indian of the few who while away,
Huddled in a rugged cañon, what remains of their marked day.

Near the *rancherias* abandoned, signs of former life abound;
Arrow-heads and curious *ollas* still in yawning graves are found;

Broken walls of reservoirs and gardens stand on every side,
Like a row of head-stones telling of the hopes which there have died.

Stands a corridor of arches, turned to greet the rising sun;
One waits for his benediction, when for us his work is done.

Through the fathers' stone-paved chambers rings the heel's half-shrinking tread,
Drear as mem'ries through a heart which knows all hopes of earth are dead.

Iron doors and cloisters bolted; rusty locks resist the hand;
What is this whose blackness threatens where the barréd gateways stand!

Dungeon sunless as the sorrow which its walls have echoed back;
Soldier life and priestly ruling, here have left a certain track.

Judge not, by the light we live in, men who wrought in greater gloom;
Leave to Him whose vision reaches from earth's cradle to her tomb.

God alone can sift the gleanings which the years have gathered in,
Horrors marked with holy purpose; good, with serpent trail of sin.

———

STANDING 'neath the bells' high arches, by the low church portal wide,
Loath, as to a home deserted, o'er the sill our slow steps glide.

Not the walls a murmur whisper, 'neath high windows' shaded light,
Of a priestly benediction, or from chant of neophyte.

Still remain with rude old carvings, rafters, choir and chancel rail;
Old confessionals grown stolid, list'ning to the oft-told tale.

No flame typifies the Presence, as the Spirit aye had flown,
And it seemed nor saint nor angel here neglected shrine would own.

Nay, behold, in distant gloaming, as the last on Calvary's hill,
Stands the Mother fondly clinging to her loved One's altar still.

And anear her Saint Ynéz the patroness of this drear shrine;
White lamb in her young arms lying—type of purity divine;

Fair Saint Agnes "virgin, martyr," emblem meet this lamb so white,
Of the innocence which baffled horrors of that curséd night,

When the loosened powers of Satan dragged thee to a place of shame,
Hoping to befoul with slanders, maiden brightness of thy name;

When grew by an instant marvel, thy fair hair to lustrous veil,
Shielding all thy naked beauty; thus did thy deep prayer prevail;

Night in which a heavenly radiance filled the chamber of thy pain,
Smiting with strange blindness those who would thy solitude profane;

Room which stands to-day a chapel, 'neath the streets of modern Rome,
Where mosiacs and reliefs still trace the woes that took thee home;

Peaceful as this lamb thy face, when for the knife the Roman foe
Bade thee gather back thy bright hair from thy curving throat of snow.

Lonely women in this weird place—watching sleepers round your fane!
Gone their broken homes and altars! guard their rest—their toils were vain!

TWO leagues distant stands the college named for Mary, as benign
Patroness of Guadalúpe, Mejico's belovéd shrine.

Sweet the story of Our Lady who on Guadalúpe's site,
Showed her pure face to an Indian, late redeemed from pagan rite;

While he wandered through the cactus, pondering her virtues rare,
Lo! upon the hill before him, stood her semblance passing fair;

And she softly spoke unto him, while he sank upon the earth,
"Fear not, son of Montezuma, chosen thou e'en from thy birth;

"Bear my message to the fathers, that a house they build me here,
And my glory shall rest on it:—Son, depart with heart of cheer."

And her smile, a radiant blessing, fell upon his spirit's strife,
Soft as sweet dew of the manna feeding with the bread of life;

Then a darkness smote his dim soul, and a dread doubt on him fell;
Thrice repeated was the vision ere he dared the tale to tell.

Spake the fathers, gravely doubting, "Lo! the winter time perceive,
Bring us now the Mother's flowers, and thy message we'll believe."

Went he forth to sunlight darkened, prostrate at his rocky shrine,
When a voice like soft air pulsing, spake in cadences divine;

Paused the smitten earth to listen, wheeled the birds and hung in air;
"Son, behold yon barren rock and thence my sacred roses bear."

When before the bishops laid he his rough *tilma* on the ground,
Stood rebuked unto their servant, prelates deep in lore profound;

On the robe of aloe thread, 'neath mystic roses piled as May,
Was the Dame of Guadalúpe, pictured in a wond'rous way.

Stands to-day an altar where her bléssed feet made holy ground,
And the homes of Guadalúpe throng the Mother's doors around.

Thus as bloom, Our Lady's legends crown the tree of faith with grace,
And peace, as their sweet aroma, fills the hearts that love her face.

But her lonely college standing 'midst Saint Agnes' goodly lands,
Token gives of slow decay, as slips the labor from its hands.

Fare-thee-well, O Mission! thwarted as a life born out of time;
Scarce had pulsed to full existence, ere was hushed thy heart-beat's chime.

On thee now the sunset reddens, dropping down from sky and hills;
Thus Time shrouds in twilight glory ages past and veils their ills.

LA PURÍSIMA CONCEPCION.

L A Purísima Concepcion—thus their faith the founders tell;
　　Tender names on shrines and valleys, read us their hearts' loving well.

Stood the Mission first to bear of Mary's holy birth the name,
One league westward from the present; to it sorrows early came.

Looked afar its goodly frontage, from the hills to verdant plain,
By the river Saint Ynéz, which hastens here to join the main.

On this Mission's natal day, the feast of La Purísima,
While the neophytes were kneeling, shook the smit earth near and far.

From the devastation of the falling walls and yawning ground,
Natives, deeming it God's anger, fled to shelt'ring mountains round.

Long the fathers sought to break the spell of superstitious dread;
Now in thriving town the ruin stands among the living—dead;

And stone aqueducts unbroken, take the river's stream to-day,
Cool and pure as first they bore it, nigh a hundred years away.

Where the Santa Rita Valley stretches to Purísima,
And the curving foothills shelter from the salt breeze drifting far,

New Purísima Concepcion raises pillared square façade,
Roof upon broad shoulders lifting; long, low, unarched colonnade.

Portal *pimienta* shaded, looks to reservoirs long dry;
Fountains gone from stony gargoyles gaping hideous to the sky;

Broad low roof, tile-covered, shelters wall which bravely time withstands;
All within bears cruel trace of many spoilers' daring hands.

Other touch than Time's has robbed it—torn the pavement from the floors,
Ev'ry sash from out its windows, and the casements from the doors.

Outraged priest his treasures gathered, when a stranger claimed the place,
And of holy churchly uses, left he but defining trace.

Tells a leaning chancel rail the spot where stood an altar, when
Floated down, like bird ill-omened, yon old gall'ry's last "Amen."

Stark as criminal forgotten, hangs the pulpit to the wall,
Yawns the earth as grave beneath it, all impatient for its fall.

Scarce a trace of pleasant living marks the row of padres' rooms;
Chill and damp and lifeless stand they as the rifled Appian tombs;

Hide the bats within its shadows; swallows cling unto its walls;
Softly slip the gilded lizards o'er the porch where sunlight falls.

But a breath of horror hovers still about the donjon keep,
Whispering of the souls that shuddered as if there they yet might weep;

Indian souls, that saw no beauty in the life they learned anew,
Yearning for their fathers' freedom, to their savage instincts true.

Lingers on this ruin's front a cannon-ball's depression still,
Made when daring natives dragged the weapon to the fronting hill;

But the gentle Mother, watchful of the shrine that named her "Pure,"
Gave to them a vision worthy souls from lowest hell to lure;

When at night they would have burned the wooden cross that marked the plain,
Lo! amidst the flames infuriate, unhurt by the fire's red stain,

Stood the Mother "ever virgin," and upon them softly smiled—
Look that would from Satan's own breast his worst purpose have beguiled;

And when died the light in darkness, stood the cross unscathed by fire;
Turned to their allegiance e'en the hearts most moved by savage ire.

Thus she watched and stayed the ruin till th' appointed hour was come,
When, as saith the ancient story, 'gainst Fate e'en the gods are dumb.

But this shrine, a lovely picture 'gainst the hillside's green is spread,
And the drooping outlines tell the artist-author—priestly dead.

Columns white stand 'gainst the darkness, in a bas-relief sun-cast,
Traced with arabesque of shadow, by the pepper boughs wind-grasped.

'Gainst the gloom, from light reflected, window-slips outflash like smiles,
As our faces beam with sunlight o'er the hearts no joy beguiles.

As a painter on his palette tries the hues his dreams have seen,
Storm and sun upon this tiled roof toy with tints of unnamed sheen;

Dainty bit of nature's trifling; to repeat her work most deft;
Fall the pen and brush presuming, of their fulsome pride bereft.

Lovely in its desolation, lies this wreck upon life's shore;
Ne'er again the earth shall call it! man shall know its place no more!

SAN LUIS OBISPO DE TOLOSA.

WHEN the fathers passed to southward from Antonio's new-made shrine,
    Just within the shelt'ring steeps which bend to skirt the sea-coast line,

Full two score of leagues their journey, as the bee his pathway grades;
Many score they wandered blindly in and out 'mong unknown glades.

While they yet were strangers in the passes of the mountain land,
Ne'er forgot the loving Master, burdens of the patient band;

Once within a deep, lone cañon, when night found them without bread,
Came toward them o'er wooded hill-side—shadowed glories round his head—

One who led them in sweet converse, and laid bread upon their board;
Found the morn their guest departed, and their hampers newly stored;

And a radiant youth oft met them, offering flask of grateful wine,
And they felt its sweet refreshment, knowing not the gift divine.

————

SOON a jutting point they chose, which would a crescent haven make,
    Lest 'gainst their poor caravels the ocean surge too roughly break.

From this spot the bold bluffs rising brace their backs against the waves,
Saying to the driven trade-winds, " Not too rude, ye ocean slaves."

On these rugged cliffs to seaward, opened are the graves to-day,
Where the unbaptized were buried with their vessels of coarse clay.

Hence a mountain-crowded cañon reaches inward from the sea,
Till it meets two pointed summits lifting heaven's canopy;

Here for Louis of Toulouse they set the bishop's crosier down,
Gave his name to dreamful valley, river, and the mountain's crown;

He who to the throne of Naples for Christ's love gave up his claim;
Who bare-footed, unattended, prelate to Tolosa came;

Ne'er forgot was the good lesson of humility thus shown,
By the eager crowds which waited, his young mitred head to own.

From this shrine by Serra's own hand planted in the wilderness,
Looked the patron on the padres' early struggles and distress.

Saw the horde of naked wretches glide from hut or hidden cave,
With the stealth of evil spirits—longed his heart their souls to save;

Looked he on two goodly rivers meeting just below his feet,
Saw the flocks yet unborn feeding on the wide plains' verdure sweet;

Looked upon the valley pierced by rugged buttes which singly stand,
Boldly stationed as a chain of sentinels across the land.

Far beyond, th' *Arroyo Grande* hills he saw in dim blue fade,
Sweeping round to meet the bluffs which here bid restless tides be stayed,

Then the patron smiled approving, for he saw the land was fair;
Far beyond its fellows prospered this young shrine beneath his care;

And soon rose the solid walls which claim their place 'mongst men to-day,
For their time the most pretentious owning Missions' youthful sway.

O'er the portal's triple arches, sweetest bells from Spain long swung;
Now in modern tower look they criminals in gallows hung.

Where the tiled roof low extended o'er a sweeping colonnade,
Now glares sun on uncapped pillars, grim as conscript picket-guard.

This the corridor historic, by the tales the people tell—
Be they verity or legend—of strange scenes which here befell;

For once paced a sad procession—grieved the morning at the sight—
Bent forms draped in sombre garments, dark against the Mission's white.

Bowed heads, with *rebozos* covered, followed where Ramona led—
Brave Ramona de Pacheco, lifting proud uncovered head.

Came señoras leading children, from a night of prayer and grief,
Seeking from young Fremont pardon for Don Jesus Pico, chief.

To their slow half-smothered footsteps, sighed the corridor's cold pave,
As they passed to the commander, blessed with power from death to save.

As of old came Roman matrons, seeking for their city's life,
At his feet knelt these untiring—stern the soldier's spirit strife;

Tolled the Mission bells the moments; paced the sentries to and fro;
Flung the sun his bloody banners; still the pleaders would not go.

Came the word to stay the sentence; "*Gracias Dios*" checked their tears;
As *alcalde* of the country, lived Don Jesus many years.

Served this corridor for barracks or defence 'gainst murd'rous band,
Or for weddings' grand *fiestas* while peace still smiled o'er the land.

Thence on festal days the padres on the gala scene looked down;
Rudest games and feats athletic, Indians' simple lives to crown;

Or when 'gainst the waving, red flag, goaded bull his fierce head bent;
'Neath his raging horns too often flowed man's brave blood, idly spent.

Thus passed years of toil and pleasure 'neath the padres' gentle laws;
Never houseless was the stranger; ne'er forgot the Master's cause.

Thronged its neophytes by thousands; o'er the hills its glad bells pealed;
When the storm broke lacked it not its martyr waiting to be sealed.

For 'twas here that Fray Ramón spent many years of faithful life;
Torn to shreds his goodly labors in the time's chaotic strife.

Driven from its wealth forth went he to a hut with naked walls,
Thence from crusts shared with the Indians passed he to the angel halls.

And 'tis said that when the hour came which should give his soul release,
Through the hut throbbed heavenly brightness and a hymn assuring peace;

And athwart the light which seemed as radiance from bright wings down cast,
Glorious face, like pictured semblance of St. Francis, slowly passed,

As this saint himself would bear, e'en to the Master's very throne,
Soul that served its fellows with an ardor like the Master's own.

And they claim that round the spot made sacred by such scene sublime,
Yearly, at that hour's returning, angel voices softly chime.

———

GONE the plaza and the fountains; Spain's delights for aye are fled;
E'en the square of consecration now receives no more the dead;

Gone the neophytes who wondered while the unknown God they praised;
Aliens till their rolling valleys—strangers hold the walls they raised.

Where were laid the Mission gardens, the young city's streets are led,
'Midst them apricot and pear tree, here and there, lift outcast head.

Long San Luis raised his staff o'er sweeping leagues' unbounded line;
Crowded now to sanctuary, scarce the patron knows his shrine.

Years agone each sacred vestige of the ancient altar went,
Every pedestal and pillar with the saints that from them bent;

But Madonnas of all pencils look from canvas old or fair,
From the Mother sorrow-stricken to the Maid with flowing hair.

Stations of the Holy Cross still tell the progress of that train,
Crowd accursed which led or followed, towards the hill of final pain;

Tell the fearful scenes which marked the sacrifice of that pure One,
Who on *Via Dolorosa* fainted 'neath Judean sun.

To this day, 'midst many strifes, the brave old walls unchanged have stood;
From them looks the youthful patron in a shrinéd solitude,

San José, his only comrade, and the fair Santa María;
Kneel before them strange new faces varied with each busy year.

Such the Mission of San Luis—died it 'midst the nation's strife;
Scarce cling memories as cerements—look its walls on alien life;

Haste the moderns to destroy them; each year breaks some graceful line,
And within is effort futile, to perceive its past design.

But without, the shock is greater—glaring paint on crumbling mould,
As a tinsel crown bedizens brow unwillingly grown old.

Sought in vain the Pilgrims for some trace to bind it to the past;
Sentiment and dreams are not where springs the young life hurrying fast.

SANTA MARGARITA.

Chapel of San Luis Obispo.

THREE leagues northward from San Luis, where begin the hills Lucía,
    Stood a chapel to Saint Margaret, she unto all mothers dear;

She who from the dragon's jaws came forth with dainty flesh unharmed,
And beheld the monster by the lifted cross, as one encharmed;

Who, with bold foot on his head, stood till the grov'ling fiend confessed
Christ the Man as God triumphant—Maid as Mother ever blessed.

Round this shrine stand oaks majestic; roofless walls alone remain,
Crumbling as a broken promise—dark as soul with falsehood's stain.

Empty hall and staring windows—friend nor foe its shape would own;
Eyeless skull which delving Years have from Time's charnel house upthrown.

Tossed unloved upon the wayside, kicked by every passing tread,
Spat upon by all the winters—thus has Life inscribed it dead.

SAN MIGUÉL ARCÁNGEL.

HALF-WAY 'twixt San Luis Mission and Antonio in the hills,
   Stands a shrine whose ruin e'en the stranger's heart with sorrow fills.

Here the rancho Paso Robles—Pass of Oaks, in legend famed,
Reaches towards Nacimiento—river thus by padres named,

The Nativity to honor—thus their faith marked every place;
This to lawless stream Salinas, makes a shallow winding trace.

Here for miles the oaks majestic lift their heads above the plains,
Gath'ring sunlight for their young leaves, and their life from winter's rains.

Dotting plains which, green or russet, spread as parks beneath their feet;
With cool oases of shadow, travelers' weary steps to greet.

Look they on the hills as calmly as when Indians hunted there,
Fearing to destroy a god in mountain's guardian, grizzly bear.

O ye oaks! Ye guardian genii of the broad leagues up and down!
Tell us of the scenes ye witnessed or with smile or angry frown.

In your tops we hear ye murmur; is it thus brave deeds are sung?
For the alien suppliants deign to speak in coarser human tongue.

Answers not your whispered cadence; is it worship blent with sighs?
Droop ye lower o'er the ruin lifted dark against the skies.

On these banks of the Salinas whose bold winter torrents flow,
And whose summer-slackened waters sink through quicksands white as snow;

Where Lucía's mountains shelter, stands the church of San Miguél,
Dedicate to high Arcángel—he whose sword burst doors of hell.

Backward braced against the mountain, faces it to morning light;
Spreads its oak-swept lawn to river; ne'er rose sun on fairer sight,

Than this place when gardens 'broidered Mission lands with varied green,
And the mountains, cattle-dotted, hemmed the peaceful, rural scene,

With the huts 'neath tiles or thatches, reaching to the water's brim,
And the Indians, gathered by them, waiting for the matin hymn;

On the stream's far marge pale willows quiv'ring at the kiss of dawn,
While beyond, the mountains bright'ning 'neath the first smile of the morn.

Now the sun would gladly hide his face from his appointed hour,
Grieving for the sight he looks on—wreck of time and godless power.

Long rows of the native dwellings still the pointed roofs define,
And the lines of broken shadows every falling shape combine.

Yon the house for Indian maidens, where they learned domestic rule,
And the skill of wheel and distaff, in the matrons' homely school;

Here the families, instructed in the marriage sacrament
And the sanctity of home life, dwelt in strange, half-learned content.

Oft their natures wild revolted at the lawless roaming lost,
Deeming toil and homely living, for their freedom heavy cost.

Yet came thousands with their new-found souls made glad in heavenly birth,
As if God would have election from all nations of the earth.

In yon white façade of arches, wreck of padres' dwelling see,
And within, find strangers' halls which knew their hospitality.

One lone bell, on rude cross hanging, stands beside the low church door,
Still its voice infrequent calls, "Our Mother blessings hath in store."

Well drawn columns on the wall and frescoes of an abler hand,
Carven pulpit, choir and chancel, show that love learned skill's command.

Long toiled hands of Christian layman, these new walls to decorate,
Gone to dust the skillful fingers—years their good work desecrate.

Dim old canvases still hanging, tell the shame of Judah's plain,
Where along the *Via Crucis, Christus* trod the earth in pain.

Stands amid old altar columns, saint with foot on skull defiled;
Thus the faith o'er death has triumphed, and the grave of woe beguiled.

Mary holds the Child ordained to conquer marshaled host of sin;
Looks on them St. Michael—he who saw the strife in heaven begin;

Patron he, with sword and helmet, on the dragon crushed, looks down;
Gone the wrath that smote the rebel; victor's face without a frown.

He who sat in heavenly councils; he by Lucifer most feared;
He in holy wars invokéd; he "by all the faiths revered;"

He who knelt to the Madonna, when her time on earth was done,
Star-encircled palm presenting, token from her waiting Son;

He the grandest, brightest of the flaming spirits round God's throne,
Stands in graceful effigy high o'er this altar weird and lone;

Upward looks, with face effulgent, as if asking, "Is it done?"
Love and valor, princely loyal, say, "Lo! thine the victory won."

Dreary shrine by the Salinas! e'en thy patron's high estate
Proves all helpless to thee, bound by will of a remorseless fate.

And they say heaven spoke its anger when this Mission to the power
That robbed all its sheep-clad hillsides, was thrust o'er in evil hour,

For a tumult rent the sky, like clashing weapons' brazen tone;
Booming like near crashing thunder—thunder to this clime unknown;

And a great shape, with a fiery forkéd tongue, and trail of flame,
Shot around and round the church cross, then e'en to the river came;

And behold! the morning sunlight blistered on a hideous scene;
Where the padres' nurtured garden spread its wealth of shaded green,

Wound a blackened trail all burnt and twisted in a knotted line,
As 'twere track from tortuous writhings of some fiery fiend supine.

But the church cross stood unharmed and traced its sign against the sky—
Sign that though man's works were smitten, truth it symboled ne'er should die.

Hold this truth, O fading shrine! 'tis all that's left to light thy day;
'Tis the soul that may illume e'en wasted lines of dying clay.

Awful silence broods around thee, and the noonday hazes thrill
With a pulse which seems a mem'ry of the life that now is still.

Fare-thee-well! such desolation seems of Time's own death a part;
Leave we thee to dreams and shadows; turn we to the world's great heart.

SAN ANTONIO DE PÁDUA.

WHEN from Carmel passing, Serra searched the land with godly fear,
Spake Saint Anthony at midnight, "I will rest by Mt. Lucía."

And across his sleep-pressed eyelids swept a vision to his soul—
Picture of a good *campiña* waiting monarch man's control;

From the ground in haste uprose he; prayed till dawn on neighb'ring height,
When beneath his hands uplifted, spread his vision of the night;

Rolling, fertile, wide cañada with its oaks a leafy crown,
Sheltered by the purple mountains, where the young fawns ventured down.

Crossed himself the pious Serra; spake he, "Brothers, rest ye here,
There build shrine to San Antonio—this the Mount of Saint Lucía."

Swung the bells by Serra's own hand, pealed they till the oak boughs bent;
Peered forth one lone savage wond'ring what such sounds, uncanny, meant.

Stayed two good Knights of the True Cross in this lonely wilderness,
To repeat their Master's story, mighty in its power to bless;

Built they bravely; the cañada laid its treasures at their feet;
Named they mountain creek Antonio, which came forth their steps to greet.

Many years the good work prospered—this of early shrines was third;
Of its vintage and its rich grains, through the young land praise was heard.

Where the vineyards grew luxurious now pass cattle idly by;
All the aqueducts are broken; stone-built reservoirs are dry.

Gone the shape of Indian houses; lost the *palizada's* place;
Of their mills and workshops busy, just remains defining trace.

Here the reverend Gutiérrez, with good works the Master praised,
Till thrust forth to famine by his servants to brief power raised;

Died he in his age and sorrow, served by neophytes alone,
Called they piteously on Serra, whose face their young lives had known;

And the faithful doubt not that his soul passed straight to bright confines,
Where Junípero receives the martyrs from his Mission shrines.

Gone the single-minded toilers; of their converts yet remains,
Here and there, a dark-hued wand'rer, stranger on his fathers' plains.

One old Indian, in a cañon, life at six score ten still holds;
Like dark mummy cloths about him, years have wrapped their wrinkled folds.

Still the padres' cloistered dwelling looks adown the garden path,
Where once sacred palm trees towered, flowers bloom as aftermath.

Grand old priest of Aztec nation—storied features rare to see,
Offered to the Pilgrim strangers, Christian hospitality.

Like some tropic tree transplanted dwelt he here in lonely pride,
Breathing but the padres' language; genius of the life that died.

Gracious showed he churchly treasures, which in varied uses stand;
Silver vessels and the vellum writ by Padre Serra's hand;

And the Pilgrims turned the old leaves, records of baptismal rites,
Marriage and all sacraments which tell the faith of neophytes;

Thick leaves of the yellow parchment bound with supple skins sun-dried,
With old clasps of blackened silver, brought from Spain with churchly pride.

Stands a silver missal-holder where the sacred volumes rest,
Dark without with many kisses, rich within with words most blessed;

Music script for Indian reading, quaint old characters defined;
Benedictus and the *Credo* by the padres interlined.

Curious chair once used by Serra; old confessional remains;
Pulpit hewn from mountain cedar; rafters dark with thousand stains.

Fathers lie in quiet sleeping 'neath the floor of sacred name;
Watch the saints above their ashes round the altar's blessed flame.

Calm looks down the patron preacher, Anthony of silver tongue,
On whose words, from prince to peasant, Europe's crowds enraptured hung;

Who the Christ-Child so adored that, while with fastings worn he prayed,
To his arms our Lord descended, as a Babe within them laid.

Mary of "Most Pure Conception" stands above on crescent moon,
Foot the fatal serpent crushing, tells the strife begun too soon.

Stand around the saints receivéd from La Soledad long dead;
In the sacristy adjoining Dolorosa hides her head.

But the noblest thing appearing in the dim and churchly light
Is a rare old canvas telling of the woes of Calvary's night;

Jesus, from the cross descended, lies upon His Mother's knee;
O'er her head the grief-smit angels kiss the blood marks on the tree.

Wondrous face of Christ, in which the love divine gleams from within,
Through the throes of flesh and spirit—anguish for a great world's sin.

And the Mother! who the sorrow knows upon that brow so traced,
That from off the dark'ning canvas, years have not its lines effaced.

Near the picture stands an altar to this Mother sorrow-fair;
Rose leaves faded and as withered as her hopes lie scattered there.

Roses die and hopes must perish, but the resurrection waits;
Spring renews its tender blossoms; hopes re-bloom at heaven's gates.

———

THROUGH these walls at mass infrequent, weirdly throbs the *Kyrie;*
From the few and scattered kneelers softly slip our steps away.

Backward looking from the portal shaded by pomegranate tree,
Take we thence a tender picture laid in mem'ry's treasury;

Sunlight on the altar streaming, from the small high windows shed,
Gilds the crucifix with glory—Mercy's pledge to faithful dead;

Priest whose chasuble recalls the cross by our great High Priest borne,
Maniple and stole—the bands at pillar of the scourging worn;

And the faith which lit this old man's face at mention of God's name,
Mounted to an awe majestic when beneath the typic flame,

Bowed he at the pyx uncovered, rev'rent lips to altar laid;
When, the Sacred Host adoring, consecrating words he said,

Shone his face like one transfigured by the presence of his God;
Thus looked Moses when from Horeb came he with the foot unshod.

Forty years this sanctuary saw him mourn its slow decay;
E'en now, by its lifted stone flags, said they o'er him, "Clay to clay."

Brief the *Miserere Nobis* when he smote upon his breast;
Long the angels' *Alleluia* which awaits him 'mong the blest.

Requiescat! pace! pace! through the dirge a joyous tone;
Alien earth, but native heaven! now his faith shall know its own.

NUESTRA SEÑORA DE LA SOLEDAD.

WHERE the plains of the Salinas lie beside that treach'rous stream,
　　Whose bright quicksands swell too often with a death-alluring gleam,

Ten leagues northward from the Mission of Antonio by Lucía,
Once bloomed gardens fed by streams, from hills diverted, full and clear.

In the neighboring heights the padres found the springs since known to fame;
Such their life restoring virtue, *El Paraiso* gave they name;

Found youth's fountain for the body, and such feast for soul and eyes
That within the valley hazes seemed a dream of Paradise.

Where *acéquias* gleamed like serpents shining prone upon the plains,
Now of reservoirs and gardens not an outlined trace remains.

Wide and lone the reach of valley, wind-swept from the sea trades rude,
Where stood shrine to Mary as "Our Lady of the Solitude."

Grand the sights she looked on when the Mounts Lucía and Gavilan
Faced each other o'er the green vale where the winter torrents ran.

Fierce th' *Arroyo Seco* rushes foaming o'er the verdant plain,
Mad to meet the lashed Salinas, roaring as a beast in pain;

Fair the fields when Spring-time drops bright flow'r-gems from her jeweled hand,
Crusting marge of spent streams shrunk to silver girdles round the land.

Drear when mounts the summer sun, the slayer of the young Spring's breath;
Lies the plain like stricken giant, panting, gasping, smit with death.

From it rises glowing aura, shrouding hills in autumn haze,
As exhaléd spirit lingers round its clay in subtle blaze.

Where the white sands of the stream beds meet and wait the winter's might,
'Neath the shadow of the mountain stands a weird, heart-sick'ning sight;

Piled in utter shapelessness lie the good walls once consecrate,
Shifting as the river's quicksands proved life to this Mission's state.

Moles and gophers 'neath the doorway undisturbed their furrows wind;
Caw the dismal crows above it; owls within, the young bats find.

Squalor lies at every portal; Desolation spreads her tent,
As if with Despair her handmaid, she would dwell there, aye content.

Walnut trees alone the story tell that better life was there,
Few and scattered mourners are they o'er the shrine they knew as fair;

Lone graves on the wide plain tell where thousands found of pain surcease;
Wild doves on the crosses cooing tone a requiem of peace.

Here Sería, faithful friar, fell at sacrificial mass—
Aged, famished, robbed by strangers—martyrs thus to heaven pass.

Round this shrine no chant shall echo, life can ne'er the curse dispel;
Summer winds with sharp intoning its funereal horrors tell.

Fled Our Lady to the mountains, and the saints who round her stood,
When the time of woe was on them, from the House of Solitude;

There serve they Antonio's altar, but in dim room ever drear,
She abides in Páduan Mission 'neath the shadows of Lucía.

Mater Dolorosa was she, when the patron saint before;
Now in unshrined exile biding Dolorosa evermore.

O THOU mournful Mother! standing, to the cross thine eyes uplift,
Where thy stricken Son was hanging when Doubt's sword thy own heart
    rift!

Vain man's cry of *Stabat Mater*, wailing down the mournful years,
To rehearse thy living anguish and the meaning of thy tears;

If on earth one knew thy woe, some mother like thyself 'twould be,
Wrung with pangs for which 'twere vain to seek words' idle pageantry.

Such with pain transfixéd stand as thou beside the struggling clay,
Dumb and lifting helpless hands in heritage of Eden's day.

And to these thou showest near the might of thy stupendous pain—
Woe supremest save the cry which rent the temple's veil in twain.

Such alone the fiery baptism which may give thy grief to know,
Thou who art the ideal Mother sacred to earth's holiest woe.

Lovely type of purest sorrow! Solitude thy fitting shrine,
For the giddy world has nothing for an anguish such as thine.

And thy face with woe transfigured tells from altars grand or rude,
How a mother's pain may be a soul's sublime beatitude.

SAN CÁRLOS DEL CARMELO.

MONTEREY of fame historic, turn we to thy changing skies,
Where the white fogs of the morning blaze in sunset's scarlet dyes;

Monterey, thou place of slumbers deeper than that sleeper knew
Who upon the storied Catskill slept his score of winters through.

Narcotized by mem'ries art thou, than the maid enchant, more dumb!
To awake thee will the prince, whose name is Progress, never come?

Nature's largess gave thee beauty; sands so white for thy blue bay
That like pearls from mermaid's necklace, o'er it seems the loosened spray;

Mountain doors that close around thee—some that stand but just ajar—
Shelt'ring from the ocean winds which sweep Salinas plains afar;

On thy cliffs the native cypress drinks the fog as man drinks wine;
Fringes miles of stately forest—live-oak and the slim-leaved pine.

On thy hill the old fort crumbles; many tales of treachery
Its dumb walls could tell of times when government was anarchy.

Through thy streets quaint figures wander—driftings of a century's tide,
Which, receding, left them stranded—lie their wrecks on every side.

Here and there a house historic, to thy paths juts all awry,
Grim behind its garden walls as if the new life to defy.

Yonder stands "El Monte's" palace, and the maskers grandly pass
Through its groves in shining raiment, courting Pleasure—coyest lass.

Stand'st thou by it, squalid village, stooping with a century's weight,
Like an outcast, blear and haggard, crouching at the young lord's gate.

Thou that bearest name of him whose sire's high prowess won permit
To be near great Ferdinand and in the queenly presence *sit*.

———————

STANDS a cross upon the roadside where Fray Serra first set foot,
   'Neath an oak of evergreen which holds the bank with rugged root.

Of its boughs a belfry made he, when his cry, "O, Gentiles come,"
Smote the echo with such strange sounds that almost its voice was dumb.

Loud their *O Regina Cœli* rolled along the unknown shore;
Muskets had they for stringed viols, and for organ, cannon's roar.

And the ocean surge its "Amen" sung with musical soft spray;
Winds rejoiced to bear the story from the shores of Monterey;

Bore they it along the sand dunes with June's burning tints ablaze;
Forests of the yellow lupine bent to whisper the new praise;

Bore it o'er the billowy hills which with their wind-piled brothers vied
In the brightness of mosaic flaming from each verdant side,

To the cañon's deep recesses where the Indians hid in fear—
Who shall know what savage forecast told them that their end was near!

Saw they farther than the padres? felt, but dimly understood,
That the white man's curse for them lay deeper than the present good?

No dumb creature but hath instincts for its own protection given;
Smote their ears the priests' *Venite* as fate's bolts in their lives driven?

But pealed forth the grand *Te Deum*, chanted in a faith sublime,
Which looked far beyond the wrecking of man's toil on reefs of time.

Yet it seems sometimes the moaning of the hopes that later died,
Mingles with the oak's dry rustle and the sob of ebbing tide.

———

SHORT remove where Carmel river loiters towards its tiny bay,
Stands St. Charles' neglected shrine, built after Serra passed away;

Named for him whose brave young voice had called The Church to keep her
pledge,
When she hung, mad with ambition, o'er destruction's giddy edge.

St. Charles, the devout Archbishop, who, when loved Milan was smit
With the pestilence appalling by whose fingers "Death" was writ,

Went bare-footed with his clergy, weeping through each plague-swept street,
Halter round his prelate's scarlet, calling all to penance meet.

Who self-offered for the people, prostrate at the altar lay,
Sacrifice for their dark sins, if thus the dreaded scourge might stay.

Pause upon the gentle hillside, view San Cárlos by the sea;
'Gainst pale light a shape Morisco wrought in faded tapestry.

'Neath Mt. Carmel's brooding shadow, peaceful lies the storied pile,
And the white-barred river near it sings a requiem all the while.

Why was name, to Christian precious, found within this lonely place,
Borne by stream which mirrored only swarthy brow or deer's shy grace?

Band of friars Carmelite, came with Viscaino long before,
Salves chanting to their Lady by this far and fabled shore;

And their name on stream and mountain brightened all the unblessed place,
As the mem'ry of a sweet smile lightens up a sombre face.

Now remains of many labors by the loyal sons of Spain,
Not a tropic leaf reminding of the Andalusian plain.

Where were roofs of tiles or thatches, roughest mounds mark every side,
And where once the busy court-yard, searching winds find crevice wide.

Gone all trace of padres' dwelling, and 'midst ruin yet remains
But the church front in its beauty, arabesqued with winter stains;

High two Moorish belfry towers lift the sign of Calvary,
Tell the deep-worn steps ascending oft their sweet bells woke the sea.

O'er the door a star embrazured tells the tale of Bethlehem,
Far more eloquent to Indian than the priestly apothegm.

See from 'neath the low carved doorway flowers blossom through the nave,
O'er debris from roof and pillars heaped upon the square tiled pave.

Natural blocks from mountain quarries mark the walls with beauty still,
And the sweep of arch and cornice show a growth of native skill;

Graceful baptistry remaining springs its roof with Gothic line,
Corners joined with triple columns meet o'er infancy's pure shrine;

Where were altars, wild doves twitter—o'er them drops the roof away;
Where burnt type of Real Presence, sunshine streams this many a day.

Softly tread the sanctuary, where the reverend sleepers lie,
'Neath the spot where oft they lifted sacrificial Host on high.

Gone the Dolorosa's altar and the saints who on it wait;
Transept of a sister chapel shelters now their sad estate.

Guards them there an earnest priest who deems their shrine a sacred trust—
He whose search in musty volumes found what place held Serra's dust.

Yearly here the Indians gather on San Cárlos' holy day;
Sad memorial to the man who would have died for such as they.

Squalid remnant of a nation, hide they midst their fathers' hills;
Wretched tale of their misfortunes blackened page of history fills.

Weirdly echo their responses for the saint they do not know,
But they know their hopes are broken, and that Serra lies below;

And they tremble when they tell you that at midnight of that day
Will arise their buried kindred in a ghostly dumb array;

Round the ruin in procession with their torches white and still,
Passing through the shadowy doorway from their graves beneath the hill;

And that Serra, like a great God, though his burial stone moves not,
Will lead them in mass majestic on the drear but hallowed spot;

With strange aspergill will scatter o'er their forms a phantom spray,
While Crespí will swing the censer through air unpulsed by its sway;

And the altar's spectral tapers will gleam on their faces white,
And the Crucifix' soft splendor fill the dark nave with its light;

Hoarse will sob the surf responsive, moan the wind in minor strain,
Mingling with the faint far echoes of celestial choir's refrain;

Night winds will not stir the garments of the kneelers on the ground,
To the voiceless *Pax Vobiscum*, lips will answer without sound;

And will cross the brows unearthly, hands which leave no shadow there,
As the forms and lights phantasmal melt into the midnight air.

Such the shadow thrown upon the *Campos Santos* 'neath the hill,
Where the rulers of the young land many graves unnoticed fill.

At this Mission long dwelt Serra—padre of the padres he;
Hence o'er hill and desert went he through his apostolic see.

Thence returning worked he humbly with the Indians while he taught,
Bearing burdens as St. Francis when at Damian he wrought.

For the hands which blessed the emblems shrank not from all homely toil,
Teaching side by side to natives wealth of their neglected soil.

Showed he, too, by dread example—torches to his flesh applied,
Beaten breast with stones and scourges—woes for those who godless died.

Grand his spirit's consecration—sweet to him the wilderness,
If to dark souls he might carry Calvary's tale with might to bless.

Told he mass at shrine most humble, not within the walls we see;
'Neath a low, thatched roof uncomely, served he altar ministry.

Like King David heaven-chosen, came he to the temple door,
Saw he blocks hewn from the mountain ere they laid him 'neath its floor.

And when fell upon his brow a shadow from the farther land,
Thitherward turned he all gladly, lifting patient, longing hand.

Seeing naught 'midst heaven's glories his pure spirit more besought
Than a "grander gift of prayer," for poor souls for whom he wrought.

When from self-imposed retreat he came forth to the sacrament,
Rung his *Salutaris Hostia*, though his form with weakness bent;

Rose his *Tantum Sacramentum* in a tone that mocked all pain,
While the voice of priests and kneelers died in tears at the refrain;

Laid he his tired head in rapture on the breast of mother earth—
Dumb bequeath of his poor body to the heart that gave it birth.

Chill embrace which he felt not, Faith's glowing robe was round him cast;
Proved he true to poverty and to St. Francis to the last;

Bore the waiting ones his spirit, and their anthem's joyous swell
Mingled with the notes funereal of the solemn passing bell.

And the boom of dreary cannon told above the moaning sea
How the earth had lost a soldier and The Church a devotee.

And the angel voices answered that The Church in heaven had found
One whose welcome should re-echo through the welkin's farthest bound.

And on earth the testimony failed not when at length he slept;
Came great blessings on the Mission e'en while round his bier they wept.

Took he up in heaven the worship which he dropped in pain below,
Swelled the glad celestial chorus, "Lo! the end of earthly woe!"

And they laid him by Crespí, the friend whose toils were sooner o'er,
At the feet of Dolorosa and beneath the chancel floor.

Lie their crypts in desolation—sun and storm upon them beat;
Stood the Pilgrims in mute rev'rence staying their too hasty feet.

And they wondered if the angels sometimes chant above this earth,
As around th' Assisan chapel sang they at St. Francis' birth.

Spake one sadly, "Though above them no grand mausoleum rise,
God knows every place most humble where a faithful servant lies;

"Though there gleam no marble tablet, angels watch the precious dust,
Unseen fire from heavenly altars marks the place, their holy trust."

SANTA CRUZ.

ON a bluff which overlooks the seaside town of Santa Cruz—
　Fairest spot of wooded coast-line which the fathers' care could choose,

Stood, as crown upon the valley, Mission to the Holy Cross;
Now for all the padres' labor have we but the tale of loss.

Here they drank of inspiration, looking forth on shore and hill,
Gathered their quick artist vision tints which here through hazes thrill;

Looked they toward the parent Mission, where in sunset's crimson haze,
Flames Point Cypress, burning city, wrapping Pinos in its blaze;

Or at morn when through the sea fogs, hooded monks those bold cliffs seem,
Then as fickle courtiers tossing pluméd crest in noonday gleam;

Poet-priests, but toilers also, for the sweeping corridors,
Where now stand the convent buildings, told their zeal in holy cause.

Throve this Mission as its fellows, and as they, knew other life—
Neophytes' rebellion and the press of Mejico's hard strife;

Lacked it not the martyr record—here by Indian hate was slain,
Fray Quintana when the midnight hid the brow with brand of Cain.

And we know that much good work was here done in the Master's name;
Rev'rence for its grand processions from us still the old folks claim.

For when day of crucifixion came with round of every year,
"Holy Cross," which named the Mission, had a special worship here;

Weirdly chanted priests beneath it the "Reproaches" of that Dead
Who to holy symbol changed the gibbet with His sacred head.

"O, my people! why my sorrow hanging on the bitter tree;
Why for all the gain I wrought ye, gave ye but such pain to me;

"Though I flayed the pride of Egypt, scourged ye me with cruel rod;
Though I slew her first-born for thee, fell my blood on Calvary's sod;

"For the fiery pillars standing behind ye at Egypt's sea,
Pillar of the flagellation, O, my children! gave ye me;

"Led I ye from your tormentors, gave ye me unto my foe;
Though I gave ye mighty sceptre, crown of thorns mocked my great woe;

"Though in deserts with sweet fountains and white manna ye I fed,
Vinegar unto my thirst ye gave when faintness bowed my head."

And the answering "*Adoramus, adoramus,*" softly rung,
Till the fervor of the worship seized each heart and halting tongue;

Swelled above the wooded hills and rolled along the chafing sea,
Till half-savage hearts were soothed by power of some great mystery.

And the Pilgrims seemed to hear the worship roll along the shore,
While old Indians told the story as their fathers told before.

So its life moved on with worship and with labor many days,
Till the never-failing hour which in the dust man's brave work lays;

And of all the fathers' labors not a house as known of eld;
Of the church there now remains a crumbling wall by staves upheld;

Vain supports too late thus offered, soon shall earth reclaim her own;
Idle as are those late efforts which would for life's waste atone.

Near it on the cliff's edge hanging cling the graves to sacred ground,
As if o'er no other place the resurrection trump should sound.

In memoriam the fathers, at the Christmas-tide still deck,
To recall the manger-cavern, th' inside of this falling wreck.

Here with evergreens and hollies and the trees of spicy fir,
Build they up a shrine to Mary and the Child who hallowed her;

And upon the Babe and Mother, look from out the festal green,
Mild-eyed cattle in dumb wonder at the unaccustomed scene;

And beyond in mimic figure, spread the plains of Bethlehem,
White sheep on their green spots feeding with the shepherds watching them;

Semblance rude of scenes immortal, wretched body to a soul,
Soul the throb of love memorial, love that lives while ages roll.

On the eve of holy Christmas, when the masses have been said,
Come the singers to the ruin midnight starlight overhead.

Ring the "*Gloria in Excelsis*" and the "Peace to men" until
With familiar sounds awakened dusty altar niches thrill;

And the hosts of watching spirits, who have worshiped here before—
Padres, neophytes and laymen—join the chorus as of yore;

And the anthem swells and rises till the heavens catch the strain,
As of old the skies first echoed on this night o'er Judah's plain.

Here the faithful and the aliens come to worship and to see,
Hearts forget their faith's sharp conflicts in one hymn of heraldry

This alone to hold the mem'ry—thus does Time our best works lose—
Of the fathers' faith and patience on the hill at Santa Cruz.

But the old men shake their heads and whisper hoarsely as they go,
"Mind ye of the time when Satan struck the Holy Cross that blow?"

Then they tell that when this Mission by the earthquake's power was smit,
As if to proclaim to man that in the book its days were writ,

From above its altar rose the Holy Cross made consecrate
By the Host beneath it lifted, in the masses celebrate;

Slowly rose and grew in splendor till its substance seemed as light,
Rose through roof and arch unhindered—shook the faithful at the sight;

Rose it toward the upper ether by hands unseen borne aloft,
Till it blazed a sight of glory through the southern midnight soft;

Fell a far and thrilling cadence by celestial voices sung,
Till the dying *Dulce Lignum* as a *Dulce Lumen* rung;

Brief space held its shape receding o'er the shrine it blessed before,
Then beyond the stars its brightness, far the loving angels bore;

And the trembling pious hasting, low before the altar found,
Holy Cross of wood down-fallen, lying prone upon the ground.

•

HAIL thou Cross of adoration! was't in Eden thou had'st birth,
  When the new-blessed parted waters found the corners of the earth!

Mystic token in that far time when with bashful hand the Morn
First enwrapped with rosy mantle young Atlantis, ocean-born.

Is 't by thee that man, an exile, keeps sad mem'ry of that land?
Or was 't thou God's pledge of peace, when Eve bewailed her lifted hand?

Thou e'er deemed by God-taught sages, emblem of some strange new life,
Since man first on record tablets wrought his faith with cunning knife;

Borne by sculptured gods and monarchs, carved on temple, shaft and urn;
Thou was't old when Egypt found thee; Persia young, of thee would learn.

Bars of death most ignominious, when disgrace was heaped on crime;
The accretion of man's venom gathered from the crypts of time.

Man's first promise to the future, in which life and death types meet;
Heritage of all the ages in thee lay at Jesus' feet.

Hail thou sign of life immortal! symbol of a death profane!
Waited'st thou MESSIAH—CHRIST-MAN, to unite thy meanings twain!

SAN JUAN BAUTISTA.

WHEN the fathers sought location for San Juan Bautista's plan
    At the twilight hour they halted near the mountains "Gavilan."

Here an undulating valley, wealth of fertile miles outspread;
To th' impatient call of ocean, happy streams unselfish sped.

Looking forth the good leagues over, with their faces to the west,
Saw they skies which might have spanned the fabled "Islands of the Blest;"

Watched they mountains blaze and fade in sunset hazes burning slow,
Till they seemed as hills celestial lit by heaven's supernal glow;

Rose the padres' chanted cadence till the night with *Aves* thrilled,
Echo leaping from her hills, with strange response the valley filled.

"Gavilans," the "sparrow-hawks," rose from the steeps in rapid flight,
Wheeled and settled on that spot which is the church's present site:

Listened they then upward floated gentle as the storied dove,
Read the padres, "Graceless savage may be tamed by Christian love."

Cruciform the church foundation, e'en the massive walls were shaped
To recall those scenes historic, o'er which heaven in gloom was draped.

Close beside where cross-formed shadow might fall on the blesséd ground,
Thrice a thousand of the faithful consecrated rest have found.

And still come in straggling numbers from the cañons wild and weird,
Dark descendants of those sleepers to the walls their fathers reared.

That which Time has dared to shatter of the structure's first design,
Now replaced and fitly shapen, lifts a front of comely line.

All within renewed and cleanséd shows the care of loving hands;
Font for rite of holy baptism, at the entrance fitly stands;

Font from solid mountain bowlder slowly chiseled day by day,
Urn-shaped vase and bowl receiving refuse of the blesséd spray.

In a choir restored the orphans, from the convent home hard by,
Led by gentle dark-robed sister, to the chanted mass reply.

And the children's *Salutaris* floats above each bowéd head,
Soft as angels' hymn of welcome drifted o'er Mt. Calvary's Dead.

And 'neath dim old canvases which show the "Stations of the Way,"
Softly chanted *Stabat Mater* tells the sorrows of that day,

When from curséd flagellations laid upon her Son's dear flesh,
Blood stains on the *Via Crucis* pierced His Mother's heart afresh.

Mounts the glory of the grand words to a transport of desire,
Bursting from a rapt soul forth, in th' *Inflammatus'* holy fire,

Still are here old altar columns; from the recessed niches' grace,
Faithful saints of many nations, bend towards Mary's pictured face;

Here stands he who on Messiah, saw the heaven-named sign descend—
Token that for herald-prophet desert work was near its end:

He the patron, John the Baptist, leaning on a shepherd's wand,
Gazes on the lamb beside him with a look both awed and fond;

Grander light his face transfigured when, to thousands desert-shod,
Spake he o'er our Lord baptizéd, "Men, behold the Lamb of God."

Halo aureate, the sunbeams, from high bars make round his head;
Through the dim church aisles we hear of buried years the stealthy tread;

Lives the rugged form before us—camels' hair his desert dress—
Rings again the cry prophetic from Judean wilderness,

And we see the broad-winged white dove rest on His devoted head,
Who anon, should be with fastings, to the great temptation led;

Awed with scenes of such grand portent, when began the gospel grace,
Backward stepping, rev'rent bowing, pass we from the sacred place.

Far the colonnade outstretches, fair and bright in mounting sun,
As life's vista to youth's vision, ere Hope's light for aye is done.

Of the rooms within the cloister, some are snatched from Time's decay,
While on some, to death abandoned, leaves his mark each record Day.

Gone the corridor to north which on the orchard once looked down;
Rises long façade to southward on the plaza of the town.

Padres' pear trees and a garden thrive 'neath young priests' foster care,
But a languishing *pueblo* dies in life-inspiring air.

Still dwells here an Indian matron strong of limb and brave of heart,
Who has watched with dire misgivings, Mission glories all depart.

"Then the rivers ne'er lacked water, easy labor gave us bread;
Is it curse, for sins unpardoned, on my people?" low she said.

Sets she forth the grand *fiestas* when *pinole* flowed for all;
Gleams her smile as winter sunbeams on the burnt, charred hill-side fall;

Tells how Indians and the Spaniards on the plaza held rude play,
Takersía—round hoop thrown and caught on canes, with skillful sway;

And Toussé, where cunning actor artfully th' attention leads,
Partner finds the hand-hid forfeit—stake, a string of shining beads;

Tells of the grand celebrations of the feasts of joy and hope,
When in lofty ceremonial, priests in chasuble and cope,

And with all the high insignia which their holy office found,
Led the faithful in procession through the church's measured bound;

Flashed the silver crucifix in sunlight as it were God's smile;
Burned the candles round the saints borne from their niches for the while,

And the acolytes swung censers till the incense heavenward soared,
Sweet as prayers of saints and martyrs in the golden vials stored;

Reverent was Corpus Christi, by permitted hands uplift,
'Neath the sign made holy by His life outpoured in precious gift;

And they bore it round the cross which rose beneath the cloudless sky,
Knelt the crowds in adoration, as the sacred Host passed by.

Tells she with dark glowing features, of the splendors of such day,
When "From out the holy Presence evil spirits slunk away."

Tells she till the list'ning Pilgrims see the dreary dark room fade,
And the plaza rise before them with the pictures she has made;

Till 'neath blazing sun they see dull altar-lighted tapers flit;
So our souls are dim before Him though from His own spirit lit;

Till through years reverberant they seem to hear the thrilling sound,
Of the *Lauda Sion* chanted softly o'er the holy ground;

Throbbing through the south air tender, till the birds take up the strain,
And to unblessed cañons bear the note of Christian love's refrain.

SANTA CLARA.

SANTA CLARA! valley lovely as a maiden basking fair,
  With her bright-hued robes about her and disheveled sun-lit hair;

Valley reaching to the southward from the broad majestic bay,
Whose name tells the world the story of Saint Francis' early sway;

This the spot of nature's choosing where her perfect work is done,
Turned the sand to gold dust by yon silent alchemist, the sun;

Where the fruits more fair than apples of the far Hesperides
To the lifted fingers drop from arms of the rejoicing trees;

Where 'midst never-dying roses, Afric's lilies boldly bloom,
Sprays exotic twine the lattice without fear of winter tomb;

Where the soft airs drift luxurious, perfumed from a thousand sods,
Till the drunken senses murmur, "'Tis the 'Garden of the Gods.'"

This the site to Santa Clara chosen by her devotees
Ere her fields of tangled wild flowers knew the kiss of myriad bees.

Here St. Francis' soldiers found the wilderness of oaks their home;
Gardens made and Indian dwellings, lifted cross and stately dome.

Here they built the Alameda which should give its pleasant way,
To the neighboring *puéblo*, th' unformed town of San José;

Planted willows right and left, which as their monument still stand;
Young and old, for this good *rambla*, bless the padres' thoughtful hand.

Alameda! fair when sunlight follows where thy branches sway;
Fair when moonbeams' silvery pencils trace thy shade in plume-like spray

Walked the fathers here at evening, speaking of this unknown land,
Shadow-like the Indians followed for the blessing of their hand;

Shadow-like their dusky outlines melted in th' approaching night,
So oblivion soon shall cover their receding steps from sight.

'Neath these skies of tireless azure, 'midst this air's luxurious balm,
Toiled the fathers at their good works through the nation's storm and calm.

Now scarce trace of life Franciscan, Jesuits the place retain,
And a strong and noble college raises here its good domain.

Where appeared old walls adóbe, modern life with every grace
Clothes the outline, as a young vine hides a gnarled trunk's ugly face.

Through the garden's trellised porches, cassocks dark pass swiftly by,
Shadows in a sun-bright picture drawn against a fervent sky.

Ripples o'er the solemn palm trees school-room hum from left and right,
As along a tropic ocean breaks a phosphorescent light.

Priestly Jesuit with guarded courtesy receives the guests—
Trainéd host, whose tact unfailing, meets the strangers' tedious quests.

By the church alone remaining with its rafters quaint and old,
Roughly carven, rudely frescoed, tale of other life is told;

Stand two altars which recall an earlier century's designs,
And a brotherhood of saints who stoop from old or new-made shrines;

From above them Santa Clara looks down on the blesséd flame,
Where new fanes or crumbling altars hold the symbol aye the same!

Crucifix with hallowed blood-stains stands against th' adóbe chill;
Pulpit quaint, no longer knows 'midst new life its old terrors' thrill

Canvas new with vivid colors, here repeats the oft-told tale
Of the Nazarene cross-laden, with the bloodhounds on his trail.

Modern windows in the old wall, like new thoughts, give ample light,
Not a corner where a legend of its dead past hides from sight.

Warm with modern life and purpose, here the present claims its own,
And the future's gracious promise o'er the shrine and school are thrown;

And the church's open portal tells the altar ever there,
Bids the weary pause and find their soul's rest in an hour of prayer;

And the *Sanctus* from the deep soul of the organ worship-smit,
Falls like dew upon the dry hearts—till the lips, with earth-care writ,

Tremble in a glad *Hosanna* to the One who loving came,
And in a soft *Benedictus* breathe their blessing on His name.

And the silent Pilgrims list'ning to the chant's soft praise and prayer
Falling on the scattered kneelers, telling *aves* here and there,

Wondered not how Mother Church, her children holds in loving thrall;
All their needs and sorrows knows she and a comfort finds for all.

Santa Clara! happy patron of the town and valley wide,
Scarce knows earth a fairer spot than where thy shrines in peace abide.

Meet reward such shrine for life 'neath scourge Franciscan, in thee, known
First to soul and flesh of woman—rest and home behind her thrown;

Thou the young enthusiast, who came on day of holy palms,
Met by Francis in procession of blessed lights and chanted psalms,

To the altar, casting there thy beauteous hair and robes away,
And received the serge and girdle coveted for many a day;

Who when loving friends from such life sought to tear thy tender grace,
Dragged the altar-cloth with young hands, clinging to the sacred place;

Who years later, ill and pallid, lay before thy convent gate,
Prostrate at the pyx uncovered, to the good Lord supplicate,

Lay until the fiery Moslems warring to thy very feet,
Deeming thee protecting angel, turned their Arab coursers fleet.

Thou who far surpassed e'en Francis in self-tortures and in prayers;
Happy vale that owns thee patron, O, thou mother of "Poor Clares."

MISSION SAN JOSÉ.

FIVE leagues northward from the town which bears the patron's name to-day,
'Mong the Portuguese and Spaniards stands the "Mission San José."

Here the Contra Costa Mountains downward into foot-hills slide,
And the Alameda Valley spreads its level acres wide;

Here above the fertile farm lands, suns the sea-fogs chase amain,
And the trade-winds blow land-tempered o'er the inland seas of grain.

In a spot where spurs of foot-hills make with warm encircling arms,
Sheltered cove from valley currents, as a reef makes coral calms,

Clustered once the Mission buildings, clinging to the gentle slope,
Dedicate to Joseph, patron—he who watched o'er Judah's Hope.

Here they built the massive turrets, houses, workshops and the mill,
All that helps to human living—Indian hands their only skill;

Here they watched the good crops ripen, and their cattle roaming wide,
From the silent brooding mountains to the distant salt marsh tide;

When from out the nation's conflicts round their heads the death note pealed,
Grapes ungathered on the hillside purpled all the russet field;

Trees they nursed bent heavy-fruited, dropped to mother earth her own,
O'er the miles of uncut harvest, in the sun no sickle shone.

Time and fell neglect have hastened wreck which human strife began;
What remained, the earthquake's fury, fiercer than the wrath of man,

Shook, e'en to its strong foundation—rending walls with bruises sore;
Nature, Time and Man united on its head their wrath to pour.

Now a decent modern structure tells the priest's returning hand,
And again his vineyards ripen where two aged olives stand;

Now one old adóbe only, dark and cool for vintage use,
Offers to the curious stranger, of the old vines' purple juice;

Round it hums a motley hamlet—farmers come with varied speech,
And the graveyard's simple tablets, in all tongues their lessons teach.

Where young avenue of olives stretches up the sunny slope,
Builds The Church a modest college as the future's surest hope.

Gone the padres patriarchal, but the modern life is born;
Dropped the trailing robe of romance for the garments of the morn.

Stays one quaint amusing custom with its story of a wraith,
By which is extort some pleasure from the rigors of the faith;

Here each year the wretched Judas comes forth from the nether flames,
Be it short reprieve or penance, unchanged still his thoughts and aims.

On the midnight of Good Friday, when the requiems have been said,
Stalks he forth as one rejected from Christ's preaching to the dead;

Takes he thus a breathing respite in the air from sulphur free,
Cooling his hot lips till morning, granted this much liberty;

But the smell of earth revives the ruling passion of his soul,
And it clamors for indulgence far beyond his weak control;

And his thieving fingers stay not till into a mound he heaves
All the tools and work unfinished, which the careless craftsman leaves;

Farmers' wagons from the roadside; casks that wait the Mission wines;
Whiplash as his pennon streaming o'er the workmen's modest signs.

While the rude pile rises darkly, and his unseen footsteps go,
Burns the greed which all consuming caused the sin that wrought his woe;

And he lives again the horror and the pangs of dread remorse,
Which to hasty gallows drove him ere Christ hung upon the cross;

And the morning sun beholds him, while the country people gloat,
Hanging to a tree for gibbet, self-placed rope around his throat;

Written will he grasps convulsive, giving to each one his own,
As the thirty silver pieces at the elders' feet were thrown.

While go on the morning masses all the youth of farm and town,
Stuff his clothes with Chinese crackers—bombs for treach'rous heart and crown;

When at length the prayers are ended, and the fire and water blessed,
Tastes he then the flames familiar in his home of dire unrest;

And the fire-crackers snapping, like the breath of hell outstart,
To the four winds, bombs infuriate bear his trait'rous head and heart.

Such the custom Mejicano and the tricks the young folks play,
With the effigy of Judas, here on Holy Saturday;

And the country people gather to the church and to the fun,
For to-morrow is the Easter, and the Lenten gloom is done;

And the Pilgrims gazed and wondered, that the city's life so near,
Remnant of a long dead century's curious pastime should appear.

Spake one gravely, "'Men are children' not yet 'of a larger growth.'"
Turned they for the Easter beauties to the great mart nothing loath.

MISSION DOLORES.

Mission de los Dolores de Nuestro Padre, San Francisco de Asis.

WHEN the Captain Portolá with his soldiers and the Frays
    Sought Viscaino's goodly harbor—so the churchly story says—

Francis by a power permitted, as they came towards Monterey,
Threw a cloud of blindness on them till they knew not the blue bay.

So they deemed it unnamed water breaking on an unknown strand,
And the holy sign beside it placed with consecrating hand.

This the "Cross of Portolá," famed for a miracle of light,
When to Indian gaze it shone like sun-bars through the forest night;

And its splendor grew and widened till its glory lit the sky;
Knew e'en unbaptizéd pagans that some mighty one was nigh.

To appease this presence brought they gaudy plumes the wild bird sheds,
Shining shells of abalone and the rude-cut arrow-heads.

While the saint thus to the heathen token gave of future good,
Passed his brave men northward through a fair but unblessed solitude;

Through long avenues of pines and level parks of oak-crowned land,
O'er dim miles of cloudy coast-lines to a chill and fog-wreathed strand;

As a just reward appointed to the meekness which shunned fame,
Showed he them a bay majestic, meet to bear his saintly name.

Call it freak of Time's weird sarcasm; call it mockery of Fate;
Name of "Poverty's Apostle," bears proud bay with golden gate.

Grandest bay! upon whose bosom navies of the world might rest,
Gently holdest thou a mirror to the white gull's snowy breast,

And thy deep arterial currents, drawn from ocean's throbbing heart,
Bear as light the iron monster or the white skiff to thy mart;

Rainbows quiver 'neath thy surface; heaven repeats itself below;
As a spirit to a substance, softer there its colors glow.

Leagues to northward, leagues to southward, wanders thy adventurous strand,
And thy sinuous arms extending gather wealth from all the land;

Wide thy Golden Gate stands open to all nations of the world;
Free between its stately portals all flags are in peace unfurled.

Beauteous Gate, when loitering sunset covers thee with burnished gold!
Mighty Gate, when surging ocean thy strong cliffs alone withhold!

Treach'rous Gate deceiving many with a name most fair to see!
Blesséd Gate where millions find the golden boon of liberty!

———

TO Lone Mountain's height ascending stood the Spaniards in amaze,
At the fair *campiña* spreading God's good picture to their gaze;

At their feet the rippled sand-dunes—billowy waves far up the shore,
Piled by tireless winds which drive their ocean brothers evermore;

Toward them swept the boundless ocean, tawny 'neath autumnal glow,
Calm its waves as when Balboa named it El Pacifico;

Alcatraz and Yerba Buena—sentry isles within the gate,
Watchword passed to picket guard—the Farallones without that wait.

Sweeping bay's oak-tufted shore lands slipped adown to meet the tide,
And receive his brief caresses e'er to other loves he glide;

And the foot-hills, elder sisters, reached around with circling arms,
Heads uplift towards parent mountain, standing in perpetual calms.

Tamal Pais—the Table Hill—sent vows on trained winds bold and true,
To the Monte del Diablo, blushing through a veil of blue.

Far beyond, the inland valleys lay like other seas outcast,
And the gleam of thread-like rivers, silver chains that held them fast.

In the spot where stood in worship these brave Frays and Portolá,
Stands a cross upon Lone Mountain, greeting sailors from afar;

And around it throngs a motley multitude from all climes led,
Borne from cities of the living to the city of the dead.

And the Spaniards, for Saint Francis, placed a cross beside the bay;
For his sorrows named the Mission later founded on his day.

Near the Gate they built Presidio, name and usage still the same;
Mission placed 'neath shelt'ring foot-hills, still Dolores bears it name;

Mission this the last to northward—all beyond no more are seen;
Scarce an Indian tells the story of the life that there has been.

Rafaél and fair Sonoma once raised consecrated head;
Now no brick on brick is standing—than a coffined form more dead.

Long Palou, the friend belovéd of the Fray Junípero,
Spent his years of faithful labor, through Dolores' weal or woe;

Fray Palou, the careful scribe, whose tireless pen to us bequeaths
Tale of faith and hardship through which great love to the Master breathes.

Now the shrine whose lands were boundless looks forth from its measured
     walls,
And th' irrev'rent voice of traffic by the very doorway calls.

Jostled by the crowding city, 'neath the hills it crouches low,
As around his haunts familiar hovers outcast loath to go.

Like an exile late recalléd, it "restored" looks on the land,
'Minding passers of the time when Indians trod the wind-swept sand.

Round it cluster walls dismantled—records of an alien past;
Crumbling roofs their broken shadows on the city pavement cast.

Huddled in a square begrudgéd, crowded lie the sleepers still,
Soon must they their rest relinquish to the greedy city's will.

Here ten thousand heads have hidden 'neath the dust earth's crown of pain,
O'er them throbs the *Dona Pacem* from the smitten organ's strain.

These small grounds are well historic; names gleam on their tablets white,
The *pueblo's* life recalling and the city's early might.

Here lie Casey and his confreres who made " *Vigilantes'*" fame,
When slow Justice, turned at bay, struck in the sovereign people's name;

Here lies Don Luis Arguello, Comandánte first whose power
Told how Mejico defied the mother Spain in evil hour;

Here the fair Concepción oft strayed, with her young face turned grave
For the lover, held too long o'er seas that ne'er a token gave.

Sweet Concepción Arguello—"La Beata" fondly named;
Count Von Resanoff, her true knight, in the Russian story famed;

Prayed she here till elfish sea-fogs wrought their chaplets in her hair,
Dark locks which were destined never other bridal wreaths to wear;

Many years unknown his death tale—traveled slow e'en warriors' deeds;
Many years of maiden sorrow—nun's pale robes her widow's weeds;

Nun the first of consecration on this pleasure-loving shore;
Dominic's white vesture hid her and her sorrows evermore.

Thus do mem'ries hold the old life to the new around these graves,
And to youth the old bells call o'er priestly dead 'neath chancel paves.

Brave young hands haste with the new shrine which shall be the dead life's
tomb,
And the old church 'neath the Twin Peaks shrinks with forecast of its doom;

Even now the engine's whistle mingles with its matin bell;
Thus th' impatient hand of Progress rings o'er storied shrines the knell.

But long years have city kneelers bent 'neath rafters dark and old,
Which the neophytes had painted with rude pigments clear and bold;

Gazed on the same canvases which told to them, with meaning faint,
Story of the Man of Sorrows—for us made with grief acquaint;

Story of that way historic where beneath the cross, bent down
Blesséd One who soon should change His thorn-wreath for His glory's crown;

Bowed they at the same old altars, where the time-tried saints yet stand,
Faces grim as if reflecting sorrows which have swept the land.

Shows the present's ruthless sunlight old and new in crude combine,
Faded *Mater Dolorosa* looks on young María's shrine;

Stands the patron at the altar with that haggard face we know,
Which saw highest love expressed in fellowship with human woe;

He whose effigies by thousands o'er all Christendom are strewn,
Rivaling in wealth and number even the Madonna's own;

He the enthusiast who wandered singing o'er the Umbrian hills,
Hailing "Brethren in the Lord" in sun and moon, earth, air and rills;

Who before the altar threw his rich dress at his father's feet,
Thence a beggar's mean cloak wearing, wedding robe for such vows meet;

Such Saint Francis' grand espousal, to his young heart's chosen bride—
Poverty, the gaunt and haggard; walked she ever at his side.

Bears Dolores name memorial for his pains "seraphic," borne
When he, lone, on Mt. Alverna, with his two score fastings worn,

Saw through hands in prayer uplifted—thus the spirit testified—
Crimson blood-stains slowly redden, such as marked the Crucified;

And upon his side a spear-thrust felt as with a sudden cry,
His cold trembling lips scarce faltered—"O my Master, what am I!"

Thus the love which sorely grieved lest it should lose a martyr's pain,
Had grand recompense in bearing sacred blood-marks of the Slain;

And his life of Lenten grief which broke in heaven's Easter morn,
Left a trail whose light far-reaching, ushered in this young land's dawn;

And to-day the city echoes answer many an Easter hymn,
Grand with clarion and organ, through wide arches high and dim,

With a note caught from his followers, whose long, love-imposéd task,
Taught their wild notes to repeat the glorious anthems of the Pasque.

Through grand chancels' perfumed airs, rare buds and tropic garlands twine,
Not more sweet than their wild lupines bound with *yerba buena* vine;

And the churchly structures lifting gilded domes against the sky,
Are the brave and stalwart children of the gray old shape hard by;

And the rich-robed worshipers who bend at Easter-tide to-day,
'Neath the stained glass o'er high altars, by Saint Francis' chosen bay,

Are the train of those poor padres, who to dunes and ocean roar,
Chanted the first Paschal service, lone upon their patron's shore;

And the Pilgrims bending with the kneelers at cathedral fane,
Seemed to hear that first chant's echo with its ocean dirge refrain,

Through the *Resurrexit's* triumph—through the *Crucifixus'* moan,
As a mem'ry through life's present beats its constant undertone.

With deep thought and mute thanksgiving for the coming of that band,
Knelt they for the Easter blessing, 'neath the raised pontific hand.

———

IN long converse spake the Pilgrims when the feast of joy was done,
"Though our faith be strange and diverse, let our meed of praise be one.

"Great the work these men accomplished with their consecrated might,
Grudge not praise to those who earned it in an age to ours as night.

"Plowmen they who broke the furrow; sowers bold who cast the seed;
Reapers we who glean the good land better for their patient heed.

"Naked taught they to be clothéd; to the idle rightful toil;
To the searchers for the pine-nuts, wealth of their own grateful soil;

"To the forest's lawless rovers, holy marriage rites they taught,
And by sacrament baptismal, sanctity of childhood sought.

"What though Indians in their service understood not all they did!
Who of Christian faith but worships mysteries in God's life hid!

"What though zeal o'er-stepped its measure! though wrongs came oft and
       again!
Is it not enough to answer that these toilers were but men?

"That great zeal which all too often numbs the heart of sympathy,
Sacrificing to a great cause individuals' rightful plea—

"That great zeal which makes fanatics whose devotion to earth's weal
Lifts the world's great causes with their tireless shoulders to the wheel."

Spake one aged, "Shows not life that, with good works, wrongs must creep in,
Long as toilers' brows are branded with the 'serpent trail of sin';

"First were darkness and confusion ere light blessed creation grand;
What from man should be expected if was chaos 'neath God's hand?"

Spake a doubter, "And the helpless! of their dark fate what can say?
Cross their shadows not our thresholds, pass their footsteps not our way;

"And the God who calls us children—e'en the lowest names He thus—
When He walks the earth at even, will He ask their souls of us?

"Dwell we in their 'customed places—build we on their hill-tops high;
If it be our brother's birthright, what to Him shall we reply?

"Or is't God's great evolution in which pass low types away?
Is't with man as with dumb creatures—lost the race when done its day?

"While we speculate they fade as sure as night before the dawn,
E'en their shadows shall have vanished ere this young land pass its morn.

"Be 't by laws outwrought so blindly when kind hands unconscious slay,
Or by pushing of the stronger—who hath wisdom let him say."

Spake one sadly, "'Tis our farewell; long has tolled their passing bell;
Naught shall answer our responses to that slowly dying knell.

"Throbs the tone adown the hill-sides, pulses through the valleys fair,
Answer back the streams and mountains, 'Lo, no more we find them there.'

"Fare-ye-well, O guardian watchers! why sit empty graves beside?
Ne'er shall come the former spirit to your shrines re-vivified;

"For the soul ye seek is risen to a larger century's life,
Life of Faith whose friend is Knowledge; Love unchilled by Terror's strife."

Long th' adieu—the love-sent Pilgrims, now with many a backward look
To the sun and shade-tipped pictures laid in mem'ry's precious book,

Turn unto the great world calling with its bold imperious tone;
Calling to its work undone and places which demand their own.

Turn the Pilgrims, but one lingers—smit with thoughts of unknown blest—
Till the hours all softly settle which have lulled the earth to rest;

And behold within the still night, when the Easter moon has wrought
Mystic silhouettes of shadow—hieroglyphs of spirit thought,

Pass by in a grand procession, radiant e'en 'gainst silver light,
Forms perceived as spirit semblance of the men of whom we write;

For Tierra and Ugarte, Jesuits from southern shore,
And Junípero, Franciscan, sometimes make this journey o'er,

Drawn from heaven awhile by love which still clings round the places where
Toiled they in the Master's service, in the Californias fair.

Follow in their noiseless footsteps other feet as shadowless,
Kino and Crespí with many toilers in the wilderness;

Ev'ry place recalls their sorrows where Fate tore their good work down;
Here they met the pagans' treason—*there* one took a martyr's crown;

And anon the voice of Serra, as they pass from place to place,
Drifts—a chant with a new cadence, while new light illumes his face.

List the heavenly Pilgrims till they wonder that their souls were faint
That their footsteps ever faltered—that their lips e'er knew a plaint.

Bids he them look down through ages as kaleidoscopic glass,
Till man's strifes and broken efforts—oft on earth but shapeless mass—

See they in God's perfect pattern; e'en dire errors but the shade
In designs, His purpose wise, from our fragmental lives has made.

Drifts the sound, "O, brothers grieve not that the old gives place to new,
That the present's rushing purpose to the past forgets its due;

"God endures to see the lily drop its petals one by one;
Shall not we abide the death of that whose work for earth is done?

"Gone our Missions' life midst conflicts, but the truth we sought to tell,
Shall resist the strife of ages, for with God its might doth dwell;

"Truth of God's great love to mortals shown in Type of holy life,
Whose humility majestic should rebuke man's pride of strife.

"Doubt not that such love shall conquer though some faith-built altars fall,
That the sacrifice was perfect, made but once and made for all;

"By the holy saints and martyrs whose great lives shall burn sublime,
Heaven-set torches ever flaming down the corridors of time;

"By His Mother's seven sorrows; by the twelve stars on her brow;
By her present adoration, in which e'en the seraphs bow;

"By His holy incarnation; by that Power which healed all pain;
By the Hand that burst the dark tomb when came forth the mighty Slain;

"By the Real Presence in the Eucharist's grand mystery,
Doubt not that the love shall triumph sealed with blood on Calvary.

"He who makes man's fury praise Him, the remainder shall restrain;
On wrath's ruin temple nobler shall uplift its fair domain;

"Temple where all hosts shall worship, waiting all saints gone before,
Militants in armor when the last trump drowns life's battle roar;

"Temple grand enough to gather all the faithful of all time;
Then shall *Jubilate Deo* blend in tongues of every clime.

"If we know not such proportions, see our measuring line too small;
Be sure God's love spans the millions as His sun shines over all.

"Then grieve not at altars broken, or at mould on cherished shrine,
God is greater than the ages!   Truth is as His life—divine!"

And the Holy Cross in blessing lifted o'er their bowéd heads
Was in substance as the lustre which heaven's open portal sheds;

'Neath its soft suffuséd glory, blent their outlines with pure light,
As at the Transfiguration heavenly forms were lost from sight.

———

CALIFORNIA, loveliest Queen of the Ocean!
   Thou Goddess in beauty's immortal array!
How long was thy sleep while Humanity's shadows
   Through thy dreams, like the phantoms of night, went their way;
How sweet was the hush of thy long sylvan twilight,
   Ere through whispers of peace rang the clash of the sword!
How cruel the shock of thy sudden awaking!
   Ere thy soul was aroused, wrath around thee was poured.

But gone is thy night; mounts thy day to its splendor;
   And thy heart-pulse is warm, like the pity of God;
Though the envious hiss with the curse of their nature,
   For the grieved of the world there's a home on thy sod.
From the peaks of thy mighty Sierras thou cryest,
   "Here is bread for the toiler and breath for the free;"

Through thy vineyards and orchards of figs and the orange,
    Thy golden sands carry the tale to the sea;
Spread thy bounteous hands to the east and the northward.
    Thy smile to the south is a constant delight,
And the fainting—thy skies and thy soft airs electric
    To new life on thy warm, ample bosom invite.

As sing we the twilight and shock of thy waking,
    More glad would we sing of thy glorious dawn;
How grand shall his theme be who takes up the story,
    And sings of the noon that shall follow thy morn;
The tale let him write with a pen of light, tempered
    In the furnace of love, and bright-tipped with the sun,
For the home of God's millions proclaims to the nations,
    "Behold ye the guerdon of liberty, won."

www.ingramcontent.com/pod-product-compliance
Lightning Source LLC
Chambersburg PA
CBHW032012010726
47493CB00007B/2365